WHEN THINGS GET WORST

WHEN THINGS GET WORST

Barry Callaghan

Little, Brown and Company (Canada) Limited
Boston • Toronto • London

First published in hardcover 1993
First paperback edition 1994
FIRST PRINTING

Chapter One appeared in a different form in Saturday Night, Toronto,
and The Ontario Review, Princeton.

Canadian Cataloguing in Publication Data

Callaghan, Barry, 1937-
When things get worst

ISBN 0-316-12464-8 (bound)   ISBN 0-316-12468-0 (pbk.)

I. Title.

PS8555.A49W5 1993   C813'.54   C93-094511-5
PR9199.3.C35W5 1993

Cover Art by JOE MORSE
Cover Design by FALCOM DESIGN
Interior Design by MICHAEL P. CALLAGHAN
Typeset by MOONS OF JUPITER
Printed and bound in Canada by BEST BOOK MANUFACTURERS INC.

The songs Tougher than Leather, Changing Skies, and My Love for the Rose
quoted with the permission of Willie Nelson Music Co. Inc.

LITTLE, BROWN CANADA
148 YORKVILLE AVENUE, TORONTO, ONTARIO, CANADA

for John Montague
who
"git thar fustest with the mostest"
when things got worst

...violent sorrow seems a modern ecstasy

MACBETH

CHAPTER ONE

IN THE WINTERTIME WHEN THE light drops to an hour so still you can hear all the elms along a road crack in the cold, me and Evol were standing at a crossroads beside a snow-bound cemetery called Primrose, out on the shoulder of the highway hitching a ride home to the home farm because we'd gone to the city looking for work only to find that no one but the quick and the light-fingered were working and there was no place there for a man like Evol who had all the grit and good looks in the world but he had no special skills, which is how the hunky boss sneered and gave Evol short shrift at the auto body shop where he tried to hire on, hoping to spray-paint busted up cars that had been welded and fixed, which he had done in the country in a wrecking lot close by Crudup's Mobile Home and Trailer Park. So we ended up squatting in a plywood shack under an old iron footbridge alongside a bunch of dipsos and kids with bunged-up brains, where we stayed right on through the month of September, the babychild Loanne with us sleeping in a knapsack like it was her own regular sleeping bag, and then when the early winter came on with that whip-snap to the edge of the wind that hits before freezing rain and the following snow, we got a room in a hostel and halfway house where there were druggies and slopeheads living down the hall, all of them deranged most of the time, talking about the molestation and mayhem they'd like to cause and probably did, so that Evol rightly said it was harebrained of us to be living there in that boarding house among people who made ordinary folk like us seem to be common dull, since we had a whole four-and-a-half room frame house, shabby or not, back on the home farm, back on our scrabbly patch of an awkward ninety acres that kept pushing up stones when it wasn't being overrun by bush.

"Them cursed stones," my daddy used to say, "always pushing themselves up and turning our people crooked and bent into stone pickers," and Evol, scrunching up his eyes over a cup of black coffee in the Future Kiev Café in the city, told me we were going to be smart instead of stupid and go home, which struck me in my funnybone, since my momma had always said before she died, "The world must be flat because no one who leaves home ever comes back," but there we were, bucking headfirst into the winter wind with Evol, though he was a loving man, taking no mind of the child bundled inside my coat against the blowing snow, which didn't please me any about him as we stood stamping our feet and staring down the dark rise of the road between the ploughed snow banks, a hollow lost feeling sucking at me from underneath my breastbone and tears freezing in my eyes since I'd never felt so lonesome and far from anywhere in my life what with the dogs howling off behind a house in a stand of hemlock, the stillness so sharp that Evol said not to worry because all clear thinking takes place only in the cold which was his natural territory, him being a man who didn't take no nonsense of any kind for an answer, not from no man, and no animals either, and so he just ignored me when I started to cry but then because an old truck had come sagging around a bend I yelled

"Is he stopping, Evol? Is he?" and he said, wagging his arms

"It's hard to see, but I think he's stopping," and then we climbed up into the cab beside a slope-shouldered and long-jawed man with darting eyes, and the moon was up by then, pale over the snow fields as we sat stiff-necked on the high seat and all the empty whiteness we could see out there through the window seemed to contain no promise at all, a stern sight to see and confront after the way things had been with us in the city.

"Just driving on to Dundalk, folks," the trucker said, "but that's better than nowhere and besides a bus goes through, and—"

"That's right, this here beats nowhere."

"I figure you gotta be crazy and half outta your mind to be standing with your wife and child in the cold as cold as it is."

"Mister," Evol said, "if I don't go crazy I will lose my mind," and Evol laughed, and the old truck bumped up into the air as we crossed a railroad track.

"That's a fine-looking child you got there."

"Yes sir, she's a big girl if you like a big girl for a baby," Evol said.

"Hell, me and my wife, we been trying for years to derive a child outta her but she just don't take to it."

"You looking for a child?"

"Matty, that's my wife, she puts her head to the floor and says prayers before we bed down, she wants a child so bad she prayer-walks in her sleep. Not having a child, she says, is like a stone that's a dead-weight in your heart."

"You like this here kid?"

"Sure," the trucker said, who I could tell was really a farmer out trucking on the side, and I went to say something after him but Evol clamped his hand to my knee and squeezed, which is what he always did whenever we got testy together, saying, "When things get worst, how are *you*?" but I warned him anyway with the slitting of my eyes and by snapping my knees together, I warned him that he could be clever and quick and play the lame wolf with this trucker, but only as long as he didn't get sly and devious with me and my baby girl, but he smiled and whispered for me not to worry which is what he always did, whispered up against my cheek whenever he was stepping out from the home farm door in all his strut, either going to the dog fights or off turkey hunting, and then he'd drop into a semi-squat with his hands on his knees like he was going to leapfrog back at me, and say, "I hear the more sin got big, the more grace abounds," laughing and doing a hambone slap on his thigh and hip, prancing off down the lane to Pandora Road and on to Crudup's Mobile Home and Trailer Park, whistling. I never heard a man whistle so. He was a whistling fool. Some men like to whittle to pass an hour, he liked to whistle and trill like a bird and while I wiped my wet hands I watched after him through the kitchen shutters until he was gone behind the weeping birch on the concession road, and then I drew the sleeve of my dress down over his old family hand-me-down hand-painted sign that we'd hung for a joke and a memory on the wall, a sign back from the time when there'd been bootmakers in his family, long before he was born: KEEP YOUR FEET DRY — BOOTS AND SHOES, back in the olden time when loggers had come from Fergus village along the Garafraxa Road to the lumber camps, and the road was a crooked trail of corduroying through the swamps, all cut and slash through the close bog, and those sweet tough boys had carried the seeds they'd known they'd need in their cuffs, and their pockets were stuffed with sprigs of lilac rooted in potatoes for the moisture and there it was, "All planted," Evol said, "planted out where the light sits like mirror water on the back of the swamp herons." The two of us crouched on a shelf-stone jutting out of the gravelside of the ravine behind our big hill on the home farm, kicking gravel loose from under the crab-grass, talking and thinning our hopes while looking for the future and how we thought it should be.

"How much you want a baby, mister?"

"Well, hell, I never thought. You mean like money?"

"The truck," he said with his own particular kind of cornering tone, the tone he always took when he was creeping up on a thought, canny and hunched forward exactly like he was crouching now, exactly like he crouched silent on the shelf-stone digging his heel down into the gravel, cutting open an apple, prying the seedcase like it was the beginning of where all things began until whatever special thought he was working on wore itself out and he cored the apple and threw the seedcase away, saying, since he was always trying to pronounce something big in words, trying to say something that would save us from the angry sorrow inside he said he felt, "When we throw our seed away no wonder we wonder why we end up where we do," but he hadn't thought that particular thought through to any kind of keen truth because the fact was we were ending up right where our parents' parents had begun, we were going back to where my momma and daddy had died, people who had stuck to where they'd been rooted down for life because no single one of them had ever thrown anything away, and had never thrown caution to the winds, but were always looking out the shuttered window for trouble, for God and his angels of rapine who came in all stripes and sizes, Joe McGreevey the crippled tax collector, Walter Skanks the banker in his powder blue suit, and so folks were careful to a fault, digging down and taking hold with their seed, trying to latch onto hope, squatting in the beginning years inside their two-room hutches with some of the families huddling and sharing their own body heat or clustered in the timber churches, chinking and plastering the walls to keep out the swarms of black flies but the flies got them anyway, fly bites festering the way they still fester to this day like stars of pus, the fever that lays down in you like an egg and explodes the way so many dreams and lives exploded, though the log barns they built to barricade themselves and the cattlebeasts from bears and wolves are still standing, standing but empty now, "And we were driven like the driven snow," my momma said, soured by all her years of passing the winter months down snow-locked concession lanes waiting and waiting until the spring thaw came, waiting through my daddy's contrariness, which is the fund of family hard times that people all too easily want to forget and let slide out of their lives now, though it was only forty years ago that all this went on that I'm talking about and there were no big yellow school buses forcing the school boards in the townships to plough the lanes, and there was no hydro either, no lights you could just switch on when it gave you pleasure or switch off when it came time to give pleasure. It was a dark time until the first spring light leaked in through the trees like a streak of spittle low in the sky. Someone was always found then hanged at the end of their rope, or a woman in childbirth sprawled dead for want of care, and the babies too were buried on the home farm, sewn into heavy blankets and put down in the bush that was still so trackless back in those days that women got lost looking for their cows or looking for the mirror in the air that they were hoping to step through so they could disappear and some were found frozen and some were never found, gone, though Armenian gypsies appeared out of the woods instead, right where the women had gone in between the birch trees, selling spice and thread and buying goose feathers and scrap iron from all of us bent over stone pickers who'd cleared the small parcels of land while always dreading any kind of sickness, diphtheria, mumps and measles, scarlet fever, chicken pox, polio, so KEEP YOUR FEET DRY meant something, meant something deep, but not deep enough for Evol, who always took a close-eyed and contentious angle to things, chewing on his anger and his sorrow like it was his cud, because he said it should have been POWDER, it should have been KEEP YOUR POWDER DRY, sniffing around the edge of disaster, always dreaming of disaster or fighting dogs, because he loved his fighting dogs, and he also loved hunting, turkey hunting, and he loved me, but his love for me didn't stop him from cutting the beards off of all the brush turkeys he killed and nailing the beards to all the doors in the house. "Tongues of fire," he called them. "I want to hold on to those tongues of fire." But he really figured that one day he was going to lose us all. He had this doom thing in him. He used to say, "The more you do the more you know there's nothing to be done." Then he'd laugh, and if he had his times of black silence he also had his black laughter, which was beautiful laughter that hovered like a black bird with a swiveling eye looking to see if there was any more darkness to laugh at, like he always did down on one knee when he was shoeing his foot with the webbed little toe into his boot with a horn of polished deer bone, "Shoeing myself into my grave," he said, "just like all the men I mind and remember who've died with their Greb boots on in these parts." But no matter how grim he got, and he could get grim enough to ghost-dance on your heart, he loved the farms around here and hated seeing them broken up, the driving sheds and the barns caving and falling in, farmers turning their lives into piece-work and second-hand jobs and going out and carting scrap junk and stacking cars in what had been their corn fields, heaps of crushed and cannibalized cars littering their land with fenders and rusted hoods, the old split-rail fences strung with hub-caps and looped little bits of chrome, and used-tire mounds piled up and then slipped and fallen all askew and swarmed over by hundreds of cawing crows, but the good thing about Evol was that no sooner did he get his snout down into this gaunt look of things then he'd come alive with a burst of abounding grace because he sure could dance, and he sure could play the fiddle to soothe the birds, which is how I first met him one day, hearing fiddle music from far away, so I went hurrying over the rise through the dwarf pines and juniper to a clearing where he was slowly dancing by himself in a field surrounded by cattlebeasts and the cattle were spotted black and white, the sky being an ice-blue that was hard on the eyes in the sunlight and I set out running at him up the hill until I stubbed my shoe on a root and stumbled and thought I saw the cattlebeasts take a gandy step forward and then a step back in time to the tune he was playing, but then the sky reeled faster until I heard, "Lo Anne," and everything at the sound of Anne was in an amber light but I said, "My name's not Anne," and he said, "I was just saying hello, and..." I saw he was standing over me, sweating himself, and he said, "You fell down, I want to talk to you."

"I don't want to talk to you."

"Why not?"

"Because I got nothing to say," but we talked all the long afternoon, and talking to each other was almost the whole of what we did all year, except make love, which I must say bewildered my momma and daddy, not that we made love, but that we talked all the time. They seemed astonished to hear us talking, almost like so much talk between us made our making love okay. "I love you," Evol said, "like a bone-weary man loves the hour he lies down in," and he was a do-right man too who said, "So roll over woman, you're up on the rise tonight," sprawled back like he was feeling loose-jointed and eased free of all his anger and free to think about how good his life could be, at least good with me. "You're up top like you're the woman you are, in charge of yourself," he said, smirking, because he did believe he was giving me the gift of giving him pleasure, "and you can have your fun," which I had, because all of my life as a lone and alone child I had made my own fun. I knew how, even when I was locked in my room for idleness, lying face down on my mattress, I knew how to make fun in my mind and to make my mind the sky the bird flew in, or the earth the worm wormed in and as a child I told my daddy what it was like to be a worm, and then I told him worms could fly if I wanted them to. "That may be okay for worms," he said, liking to keep a hand on me, "but you can't blow your nose if I don't want you to." Years later when I asked Evol if he believed I knew what it was like for a worm to fly, he said, "I'm a believer and I know how to believe. I just got nothing to believe in," and then he rolled over and looked out the window, leaning his head on the white painted sill, the white paint flaking off though my momma had painted it with good semi-gloss in the weeks just before she died, painted it while crying that she could see daddy's face in the sink water every morning in the bathroom, which meant she couldn't bring herself to wash. Wherever it was that she looked into water she saw his face and got all confused about him, saying on end that he was going to die by drowning in the grace of the Lord, when in fact, there he was, he was sitting right opposite her, growling, mumbling that she had turned crazy as a loon, so it turned out that she lived through her last months unwashed and smelly and scented with cologne, haunted by his eyes, she said, his eyes hungering for her in the water, hungering sometimes with lust and sometimes with anger, and Evol lay with his head on her windowsill like a boy-child who'd gone early to seed, so sad, and sadder, as if it had rained all afternoon in his heart and he couldn't go out to play until the moon came up pale like a piece of wet paper and he said, "My own daddy had the gift, he was a horse trader and a handyman, good at building barns, who saw visions, an ebony-boned female demon and a cross dragging its slow length along the countryside big enough to crucify us all, redeem us all, but because my daddy's cock went dead on him after I was born, my mother believed their only hope of reaping an inchful of eternity was through me, her child who would beget a child who would beget—"

"The truck, you telling me you're willing to trade that child for this here old truck?"

"Sure," and I could feel the trucker get all tense in the dark, gripping the driving wheel hard, sucking little mouthfuls of air.

"That ain't right. Naw."

"Don't your wife dream about it, her stone in her sleep?"

But the trucker started bawling out about how wrongdoing was getting too civilized, how you couldn't trust to a world where trucks were traded for children and rape went unpunished, and Evol sat for a long time in silence listening to that trucker hacking for air, a silence so cold I knew Evol could only be thinking clear as clear could be, in the same way he'd sit beside me staring out the home farm door at the twisted pines down the lane, thinking, thinking, as grim-faced and desolate as he dared to be, all the despair in him dancing in his eyes, since he knew for sure that he could trust me, trust me to let him be as alone and haunted by the sorrow inside himself as he wanted to be, because I was always there and I always came up unafraid by his side, sometimes finding myself laughing out loud for no good reason, laughing at him and his sulks and sorrows. Sometimes, I'd sing him a song my daddy taught me. Daddy had his own way of teaching songs. Till I was fourteen, I'd lie down in the evening with my head in his lap and he'd teach me the words to songs. All kinds of songs but he wouldn't teach me the tune. He'd say, "Learn the words, make up your own tune." I never did know where he learned all these songwords, but I ended up being able to sing all kinds of songs in any old way I wanted which is how I sang at Evol, in the way I wanted

> *The whole world's worried bout the atom bomb,*
> *No one's worried when Jesus'll come.*
> *But Jesus'll come,*
> *BOOM*
> *Like an atom bomb*

16

and I laughed and Evol laughed and waved his arms
like he was letting something inside himself get free,
just like I'd laughed and waved at momma and daddy
on the day they died, laughed because they were
laughing like the loons do when they break water on
the lake, the loons who've got the gift of the devil's
laugh, which is the word the oldtimers gave the loon's
call, the devil's laugh, but Evol said the sound of the
birds calling across the water was more like opening up
a place somewhere beyond words, "On the other side
of the glass, on the other side of the silvering," he said,
"where the dead wait to talk to you, all of them sitting
cross-legged in a hole that's a great big gap in God's
mind like someone, St. Jude maybe, took a cleaver to
His thinking and cleaved His brain," and I said the
only hole I could call home was the place down the
road where our very first settler folks had set down the
first village, lightly and gaily calling it Hole-in-the-
Woods, with their sawmill on the corner, a post office
and the mail carrier, Plumer Dewan, who'd owned
good horses and was Evol's grandfather, and a grist
mill and a hangman who had two roan geldings and a
hansom cab, and two black men, the Souche brothers
who'd come up from somewhere in the southern States,
being the local honey dippers who lowered their long-

handled spoons into the cesspools under the outhouses, carrying a sign on their cart: SANITATION IS SALVATION FOR THE NATION, and they were also sweet singers singing at the first wedding that took place around the Hole because George Tullamore came to the door of grandmother Maggie Brodie asking for work and Mrs. Brodie said all she could do was offer one of her daughters as a wife, which George took, having nothing else to his name, and also she gave the wedding dinner, grandmother Brodie making sure to tell me of the fresh fish and potatoes boiled in a sugar kettle, raspberries and scones, and then she said their son, my daddy, whose nickname was Wishbone because grandmother said the whole of her life was just a wish on a bone and that's how come she gave daddy his lasting nickname among his family, my daddy who ended up so curt and counter to everyone because I figure none of his wishes had come true, and so because nothing had come true he couldn't stand contradiction. He'd gone to the school the Brodies built with a bell on the roof where the teaching all through the years and up until the thirties was in Gaelic as well as English until the second big war drew everybody able-bodied off, leaving momma and her jam-preserving and knitting kind of women behind just like they were silt, and cold winds blew off some of that silt, building up dust in the bedroom corners and dust in the crannies of windows and many bare big stones upstanding in this gravelly land ended up standing in dust, but the schoolhouse and the bell are still there, though Hole-in-the-Woods is long gone and ploughed under for the government placing of a hydro pylon that is right now standing on a little island in a springwater pond, the village long gone and leaving behind only wide open space, most of all in the winter when the winds glaze the snow on the hills to look like sugar icing on the snow and curtains of blown snow blot the sun into a red wound between the black trees, the black corduroy bark of the sugar maples dusted by frozen snow and the sky a pewter color like grandpa's old spoon.

"I want this truck."

"Right, but I couldn't live, and neither could the baby, without this here truck, because our damn farm's not worth nothing, the bloody Mennonites are buying up everything for themselves," the driver said, shying away from Evol while I hunched my shoulder into him so he'd know that if he was playing some weasel game with this guy, then he could count me out, since I wasn't no damn fool deranged enough to trade my baby for a truck, but you never knew what Evol was up to, you had to keep a keen lookout on his left hand while he was working you over gentle with his right, so we all just sat silent and stiff, listening to the rattling motor making a sound like the fan belt was loose, and the child was whimpering in the dark though the dark didn't bother me because me and Evol had always got along in the dark, defiant of the dark, and our defiance, he said, was the one true strength we had, testimony to our being unafraid to walk blindfolded throughout the house in the dark, unafraid of ghosts or the newly dead, or each other, him with his turkey gun racked over the bed, both of us listening for prowlers or maybe an ebony-boned female about to step out of his father's dream vision, though I told him no one was damn fool enough to break in on us to steal something because there was nothing to steal, and he said, "That's right, except some people would steal the time of day," and he turned on the TV, staring, sinking into that stunned silence that seeps like drainage water into your brain while it's being swamped by all those TV pictures of faces as polished as a pebble, heads talking and yammering and being pleased as punch about how awful

everything is, the kind of stuff my daddy loved, or
even better, loved to hate, flashing their phone-in numbers and prayer numbers on the screen so if you are ter-
rified and lonely and want someone to send you a
prayer cloth and pray with you over the phone, there's
the number, and Evol laughed and sneered at that TV
prayer business, saying there was only one way to look
at preachers and politicians and that was down, so far
down until you were looking at the sole-side of your
shoe which is where the shit is, so I knew why both
Evol and daddy called them all shitheels, but one night
when a big roly-poly woman with wide-open owl-eyes
said she was a psychic and you could phone in and
find out your future, Evol leapt up and dialed right in
to her and whispered into the phone and then he sat
stock-still, listening like he was a hard of hearing person, completely concentrated, and then he hung up real
smooth and gentle and picked up his gun and touched
the barrel-mouth with his tongue the way some folk
wet a pencil and said there comes a time when you've
got to abandon your principles and do what's right and
you have to get rid of what you don't need no more, so
he shot out the old Zenith TV saying he hated it more
than anything because, he said, stroking the barrel with

his forefinger, "It glues you up and gluts your mind, it glues your mind to a whole world of guff, the talk talk talk talk crap of politicians and preacher simps and salesmen," and he put the gun away and started to whistle while I said, because whistling usually meant he was on his way out the door, "We should always lie here naked and let the calm lick at us in the dark because it's the light that hurts." He rested on his elbow and I could feel the angle of his body against me, and he said, "The dark's as true as a grieving woman." Then he sat up on the edge of the bed and played his fiddle for me for so long and so mournful I began to laugh and we made love, his body like a glove, a glove that had held me warm all the way home, yet the hand inside, the hand that held me, I didn't really know that hand at all, I didn't know it at all, though I was dead sure that his dying words would be what he always said

"When things get worst, how are you?"

"This is it," the trucker said.

"Fine."

"Yes sir, you climb down here," and the driver agreed to step out into the dark and walk us back a piece to show us how and where the bus to Owen

Sound would probably come by within the hour and as he lifted his arm to point into the dark, a black steel wrench caught him on the back of the neck and he dropped, his head twisted, and Evol rolled his body into a culvert.

"Jesus takes us one by one," he said, and then he crossed himself because that's what Catholics do and said he didn't mean to kill him, he only wanted the truck, and he smacked me on the shoulder because I was crying again and shaking, and he said, "I said I didn't mean it and what you mean is more important than what you do," but when we were back in the truck driving northwest with the child between us, I burst into sobbing

"We're gonna get bad luck, I just know we are," so he drove and stared straight ahead because he was so good at staring like that, staring like he was absent from the place where he was and he said staring soothed him, particularly the way he could take a fix on a flame and look right into the blue eye-hole of the fire like he did with the wood fires he made inside the big fieldstones of our front parlor fireplace, stones that had been set so perfect by John Shearer the mason that they floated weightless and I felt, since those heavy stones were afloat in the air, nothing should or could go wrong in front of that fire, but "You watch," Evol said, "birds'll come down the chimney in the morning because cold ashes call a bird down and a bird in the house means a death in the family," but why, I wondered when he talked that way with the same grim surety that my daddy did, do men like to call down on themselves all the omens of their own dying?

"Because there are people dying who've never died before," he said and laughed.

"As luck would have it," I said, just as a police car with the whirly-gig roof lights flashing pulled us over and I screamed and screamed and screamed. "I told you. They know, they always know."

The two cops hauled Evol out onto the road.

"I traded this here truck. I didn't do no kinda rape. You want me for rape, I ain't gonna rape no old lady, I never been to Couchiching. I told you, I never been there, it must've been somebody driving a truck just like this who looks like me and you can't leave my woman alone here, she's got her child," but they sure as hell left me alone, plunked down in a short order café in a town close by called Knock, a cross-roads town of scrap dealers and welfare folks hunkering around in their shitkicker boots, singing *Take This Job and Shove It* like Waylon Jennings, and me and my baby, Loanne, we both stood there with me snuffling and her screaming but the cops took no heed as they cranked their siren and drove Evol off in the dark to Couchiching which was a lake town to the northeast we had never once passed through, a couple of cops who wore blue-tinted sunglasses with silver rims. I said, "What about me, I must have been there too," but they just sniggered and took Evol to Couchiching so he could go eyeball to eyeball with some bed-ridden half-blind old lady, and I have always been rightly afraid of the blind, any blind woman's eyes, all spittle white in the pupil, shine and color of the end of things, the shine of the underbellies of dead fish, and the old lady she said, "He did it, he did it," so they decided for sure that he did, and two days later I came to see Evol who was bunked all alone in the Couchiching jail, which was a small red brick squat place if you looked at it on the outside of the building and all shiny enameled cinder blocks on the inside, bright bright cinder blocks with fluorescent lights overhead to really light up all the dark brooding and thinking that was supposed to be going on in there, except Evol said he was the only prisoner because there weren't even any drunk drivers, making the place seem empty and abandoned and certainly not ripe with his kind of wrong doing, though the police had not yet put two and two together between the truck and the dead driver who was probably still in the culvert and all Evol could figure was maybe the wife hadn't reported him missing, or maybe she was glad to get rid of him, or maybe he had no wife and he had actually stolen the truck after raping the old lady, all of which left Evol with that unsettling sly light he always got in his eyes before he went hunting brush turkeys, sitting with a sideways winsome tilt to his head like his head was half cocked outside of the world, and I could see he was starting to circle down inside his own head, listening to some silent music that was all his own, when he told me

"But after all is said and done the only consequent thing is that I don't think hardly at all about what happened, or how, or why, or about the truck driver. It was just worse luck for all of us. Worse luck, that's what my daddy always said. Worse luck needs no blame, because the laying of blame is for those who can afford it or are born to it, like hens get born to lay eggs. It comes with the clucking."

And he laughed, a strange hardly breathing low laugh from the back of his heart, like I've heard him laugh right after he's fired his gun.

"It's the joke that gets me down, that's all, the joke of that scrawny old blind bitch of a woman braying at me about me being the one who knocked her down and then she said that I did her, splayed, she said. 'I was splayed,' and the guard, you see him? He's a goddam sweating porker who's got these here rumples of corduory fat on the back of his neck, and he says they're going to fix a peckerwood like me, grind me down to a tiny nub of stone with nothing to do but clatter around in God's headbone, a dry stone in a dry pod, like a baby-child's rattle, that's what he said, and I was thinking all night that God's mind must be like that, a child's rattle full of dry laughter, so all I can hope is that Loanne, whenever it happens that she's able to get close to God, why she'll rattle and shake some sense into His ear but it won't matter none to me because by then I'll be long gone as a bead of light,"

and he stood up and then sat down and winked and said, "You remember that TV psychic woman, she said as bold as brass to me, she said, 'The life you'll lead is all your own, and the life you take will be your own too,' and he smiled as benevolent as he'd ever looked at me, full of a kind of dark sheen, as if the dark could glow, as if inside the night itself there was a light, a seed of light that was always alive so there could never be a total darkness, and listening and looking at Evol, I suddenly believed there was a whole world in him beyond what I'd ever known, or ever could know, no matter how close we'd been, no matter how we'd cradled into each other, and he seemed like he'd already gone away from me, beyond any horizon we had ever dreamed of, beyond the steel bars where the moon-faced guard's head was suddenly poking, whining at us, all in a sweat, "No more time, you've run out of time," and before they could haul Evol into court to try to hang him for what he didn't do, he hanged himself in his cell, I guess for what he did do, which sort of dovetailed his life because he always did have a hungering for death, almost doting on death, the way he suddenly blurted out to me one day, "I am an accomplished man, that's what the dead man says," I guess getting rid of whatever principles he had so he could do what he thought was right, and he probably did it as calm and subdued as we'd been on that sunny afternoon when I laid down sideways on our bed to sort out my little boxes that I kept for his shirt studs and tie clips, but also, those boxes were filled with dried wild flowers, the white petals of field daisies that curled around the dark heads, heads like pin cushions, which I also collected, and hat pins, pins for my hair, old pressed-glass jars and satin sofa cushions with needle-point names in fluorescent thread ... Loanne, Evol ... and my momma's name, Sabina, my sad sad momma with all her old tonics for the sleepless nights

the same heavy load of sleeplessness that I had to stare wide-eyed into while lying in bed hungering for Evol after he died, and I still did miss him, desperately, and I did need to hear his voice, but I remembered how my momma had told me to hold two small flat stones in my mouth until any and all dread abated, so that you took the weight of the dread in the mouth and not in the heart, a weight which you could then spit out so the dread ended up becoming only a daily drone of emptiness, a drone that had hold of me by the heart strings because toward the end of spring my baby had also gone down into nowhere, my Loanne, a child born flushed and feverish, suddenly taken to bed by the whooping cough not a month after Evol was buried, and she was a real honest-to-God whooper though they said it was pneumonia, my big-boned baby girl going blue-faced from too small a heart, so the doctor told me, and she hung on and hung on to her little life, but at last gave out and the day she died was a terror, like a long-tailed cross dragging itself over my heart, a worse pain than when I buried Evol, because I really did feel on the day she was lowered down in the June heat, I did feel that some live thing ticking inside me had stopped, just stopped like a dead clock looking as empty as a dead clock looks, so in a yearning kind of way I didn't want to ever let go of the ache of that emptiness because the ache kept the echo of her alive in me, which was a consolation, like whenever I needed to get consolation from the ache of the absence of Evol I went out to our old clearing, ducking through the dwarf pines and junipers and I talked to him inside my own mind, wishing he would talk to me, out there alone among the trees that have got their roots curled and humped out of the ground and one time I saw a spider in the throat of one of the roots which I took to be a sign of some new on-coming grappling in the heart, so I up and swallowed mother's tonic for the blood along with my Orifer Multi-Vitamins, swallowing hard on her sulphur and molasses, and I had all her other remedies too for ills and aches, my best being for

Done Feet, taking one tablespoon of salt, one fig of tobacco, one pint of urine, all simmered and sponged on at bedtime, which was always good for a big laugh because anybody I knew of in town or down at Crudup's Mobile Home and Trailer Park, who was brought up with any brains at all and watched TV, was busy popping all the pills that they'd seen sold on television, Carter's Little Liver Pills and Templetons' TRC's, and Tylenol and Excedrin, but Evol's cure for done feet was the best of all, and that was to sit down and do absolutely nothing and drain your mind of all distraction, an entire draining until this light that was not a light you could see anything by began to well up in your body, a light like you get when you close your eyes completely shut, shut tight on a bright summer day and you stare up toward the sun, and all that heat is full on your face and there's suddenly a bright light inside your eyelids but you can't see anything except your own little veins across the light. You just know there's heat alive in you, the same way Evol came alive in me, and Evol also had his very own cure for the deadfall of loneliness too, because he'd say

"You just squat yourself down in the woods with a deck of cards and lay out a hand of solitaire on an old stump and sooner than you can say the word Solitude, somebody will lean over your shoulder telling you to put the Black queen on the Red king," Evol laughing and getting down on his haunches on the hillside that was ripening with rapeseed, naked and wearing only a long greatcoat in the spring, with tufts of sweet grass under the wild plum trees and pine cones that had fallen last year like charred birds with circles of windblown sand around their skeletons, and small white fists of flowers growing between the skeletons, and Evol said, "In the years gone by people were luckier, they knew that when awful things were done there were demons all over the place, creatures with eyes instead of breasts and one with only a huge foot and he slept in the shade of his foot, but we've got so damned well smart about ourselves that we no longer know who the demons are. Keep your eye on the owl. When he closes one eye he's the killer no one sees. The owl's got his eye on us. We can't blame anybody else for what happens, we can't blame anybody else because we've created death." He was sitting in the brush willows like a bird-watcher, except his eyes were fixed on a clump of clay as if he'd found a clue down there between his feet, a clue to what was troubling his mind. "It gets so bad," he said, "thinking about your own

thoughts, that you can hear birds walking inside your
own skull," and he was expecting me to be surprised,
but I said birds inside your skull is nothing new to me
because my grandma who'd married Catholic told me
all about it, how the Holy Ghost had come as a bird
who flew right to the inside of Mary's head through her
ear and the Holy Ghost's words were His seed and
what He said was the Word, and Evol said that that
sure gave a whole new meaning to birdseed and bird
calls and all the seed of all the birds calling around us,
all the hawks and buzzards and bobolinks and redwing
blackbirds down by the stream behind the hill, a stream
we'd dammed to make a wetland, a shallow black-col-
ored lake full of stumps and fallen trunks where the
brush thickened, always thickening around us, claiming back what was cleared years ago, the stones and
gravel pushing up as fast as Hole-in-the-Woods and
Sackett's Corners disappeared, and trying also to claim
Mount Zion church, though I hadn't been in it for
years, but had only seen it across the road from the
trailer park, the brush claiming the old closed-up cemetery and all those bones of our people who'd been sent
back into the land, the cemetery cornered and confined
by the growing junk pile fields and mobile homes

jacked up on concrete blocks behind them, fields that became a smear, an ugly wide snail's smear of what's becoming lost to us all, the sweet land and the scrub land also gutted, with Evol lost and my child lost, my sweet Loanne who we'd called Loanne because of what I'd heard Evol say the day I first saw him when he said, "Lo Anne," as if that was my name, so we'd made it hers when she was born, but now all I had was the things bequeathed to me, the boon from my momma and daddy, this scrabbly patch of farm with its gravelly hills and mounds that sometimes seemed to be a place where all the birdseed had been aborted and all my hopes abased.

This farm that was nonetheless the nearest I could come to the breathing lives that were lived and long since forgotten around here, and when I wanted to get close to those who were forgotten I walked back through the woods following the markers in the map of my mind, walking a branch of the Saugeen in the shallows, flushing chipmunks and flickers and a hare, until I got to a closed-off stand of gleaming white dead elm trunks in a marsh that Evol had found for me, a blind in the woods that had been flooded out one year by beaver dams but now it was dried so the ground was

covered by a thick weave and braiding of bleached
rushes and long grass, a windless place, the black water
in the pond just past the marsh heavy with lilies and
floating pollen and wrecked drifting trees, and dragon-
flies pocked the air and some days I'd sit there till it
was night wondering how far beyond welfare and the
little bit of life insurance left to me through death, how
far was I going to be able to go to make the ends and
intentions of my own life meet, but still I felt calmer
than ever before, strangely consoled by everything
wrecked and windless around me, like it was a stillness
of angels, and I remembered my daddy who'd always
felt cornered telling me his favorite song

If I had the wings of an angel,
Over these prison walls I would fly,
I would fly to the arms of my darling
And there I would willingly die

and then he always said that all he really wanted was
"to get out of this world alive" but it wasn't until just
after Loanne died that the foundation at the corner of
the house suddenly showed up sopping wet, what with
underground water sweating through the stone, and

Burly Crudup, who'd built the mobile home and trailer park down along the town line road where Evol had sometimes worked, Burly came by because he is a witcher, carrying his apple branch, and he set to witching for the water. It wasn't till then that I truly felt in my marrow how much I longed to be here despite all the deaths now fastened to me and to what he rightly called my crabbed land, watching the branch in his hands wrench and dip to the earth and he said, "There's a crick, a source down there," and he handed me the branch, saying just like Evol had said about his daddy, "Some have the gift," as I held it out from my belly and it whipped down and the bark tore in my hands. "I mind you don't need me," he said, "least not to tap into your own springwater," laying his hand soft-like on my shoulder, and I laughed and laughed and the next day I walked the whole puzzle of clearings, crisscrossing and tracking the veins that were a web of water, reading the map of the land's body, and later in the evening sitting at home watching the fieldstones float weightless in the air around a fire in the fireplace, I felt at last a real yielding to all my scrub acres, a yielding to my own stone picker dead, like I was saying a prayer of sorrow that made me joyful, a prayer for my own poor child who had shed this world with a whoop, and for Evol too, who was always trying to get the hang of things so he could have his way with how he lived, have his own sweet way with his own life, which is what he did at last, creating death where he stood, but the place I had to stand, planted now on my own two feet, is where I learned exactly how I am when things get worst, because I learned that a grace abounds in the earth where darkness lies and is held in a crystal web of water, a web that I can see clearer than clear which means the light in my mind is as cold as cold can be.

CHAPTER TWO

IT'S HARD TO GO FORWARD WITH death always in the back of your mind and death had been in my mind ever since Evol went down, leaving me sitting by myself for weeks after he died, sitting snailed up in a corner of the sofa staring into my baby girl's eyes, seeing a glint of softness, a deep softness in the pupil that I knew was also a softness somewhere inside myself, a softness cocooned and lying low in me but upcoming, I believed, like Loanne always came up with her fists in the air when I kissed her, just the very same way I'd done on the first night I lay with Evol, lying easy and open to him in the dark, except suddenly I put my fists in the air in his face, and he kissed my knuckles the way I kissed my own child's balled hands. But then Evol had hung himself dead, and some weeks later Loanne came down coughing, her nose bleeding, blue-faced in her bed and starting to shrink up like she was trying to disappear from her own pain but she hung on and hung on, and I wished and wished my momma and daddy were alive to help me, until I stood there on that last day in the bedroom with her and I was scared so still that I was absolutely sure someone was leaning against the door to the left of me, watching, a woman watching, and it was no one I knew though I had a troubled sense of having seen her before, like a shadow face on the other side of a dirty shop window, but then I wondered whether she might not be me long since grown old and now here she was come back through the silvering and I wanted to reach out and say help me, and touch the woman on the cheek, but the blood was all over Loanne's sheets and over her face, so I picked her up and ran hollering out through the screen door, banging the door on its hinges, and took off down the lane, running toward Pandora Road, and I remember the sky full of pollen and seed flecks floating thick in the air and I thought they must be the souls of all the angels come to see my baby die as I slammed right into a man standing lanky and tall with loose blond hair who was holding his own elbows and leaning against the fender of his half-ton truck under the basswood shade tree like he'd been waiting for me the whole time, his intention, whatever it was, a seed under his tongue, and that's what I heard in the back of my mind

"This man is intended,"

so I hauled up into his truck and he drove, side-swiping a couple of saplings and slamming down the mail box along the lane and then he veered hard to the right onto the town line past two twisted pines and a black horse and carriage, with a Mennonite driver sitting under the black circle of his big hat between the pines, until he ended up cutting through Crudup's Mobile Home and Trailer Park gates, taking out some fencing hung with hub caps and old license plates so that Burly Crudup stood bawling after us, but none of this made an inch of difference or delayed the dying because Loanne let out one last cough and a mouthful of blood in my lap and then let go of this life and me.

"Jesus H. Christ," he said, skidding on the soft shoulder of the back road into town. "Jesus H. Christ."

I didn't know how to do anything except cry, which every nurse in the town hospital said was exactly the right thing to do, though it seemed to me all wrong, standing bare-faced like I was in front of the fresh painted walls of the children's ward beside a man I didn't know who was scowly-eyed and reaching out to touch the blood on my baby's lip, saying, "The blood of the Lamb knows no evil," while up there on the wall bigger than life was Minnie Mouse in her clunky shoes kicking up her painted heels. Loanne lying there dead in that cartoon room was wrong, like Evol dying the way he did was wrong, deserting me. That was wrong as wrong can be. My momma said all through my childhood that two wrongs don't make a right, "But a whole bagful of wrongs," she said, "make up most of a person's life," so I figured I was left holding the bag and it was a bag of hammers. I stopped crying and made a hand-circle of a blessing in the air over my girl's head and the guy with the half-ton truck, who's name I still didn't know, he knelt to one knee and said some kind of prayer into the hand he had clamped over his mouth, and then he was polite and said he'd look out for me and drove me across town to stop and pause by Sparkles Bar out by the new industrial league hockey rink, but I said, "No, no," so then he stopped in front of St. Jude's church with the tilt to the steeple from last year's tornado, but I said I didn't want to deal with the ghosts of my dead momma and daddy, too, who'd been buried out of that church, and I didn't want to deal with the dread that always clings to the walls in the silence of an empty church, and I said, "No, no," and he shrugged and said, "Prayer's a private and rapturous thing anyway,"

and drove me home and not only didn't go away to wherever he'd come from but hung around all afternoon, standing there gangly and awkward on the porch while I shuffled in and out of rooms, dopey-like and dazed, and I decided to let him be there in the house only because I was afraid to find out how I'd do all by myself, alone, so he told me how his name was Luther but I should call him Lute, throwing his long leg over the arm of the porch chair, and he said he could see how I was all alone, and he said how he was the A-number one hardware man in town and how he'd inherited his father's business, Avery Alm's

Hardware, and I knew it to be a dark green store down
by the 7-11 on Finnbar Road but I had never been in it.
He also said he was a come-by-chance preacher, because
one day he'd opened up his long deceased mother's
Bible, and had taken the chapter and verse numbers
from the top of a page in Deuteronomy and he'd pen-
cilled them in on a red and white lottery chit in the
Mac's Milk Store. He'd won ten thousand dollars in the
lottery, so he figured that numbers and the holy Word
had come to be a blessing in his eyes, a blessing he was
bound to carry forth, not only into his business doings,
and he said he was going to do some serious business
with me, whatever that could be, but also it was a blessing he carried into the small yellow brick sideroad
church that he'd bought and taken charge of at the gate-
way to the old cemetery, and I realized he was talking
about Mount Zion across the road from Crudup's
Mobile Home and Trailer Park, a churchyard that was
full and in some places double-bunked with all the stone
pickers from our families under stone markers in the
yard, my momma and daddy among them, and he said
he'd reclaimed the chapel from the wrecker's hammer
and reclaimed it from the past because he was a man of
the future, definitely of the future, and he now called it

the Chapel of the Abandoned Apostle, a chapel he kept open wide on Sundays for people mostly from the trailer park who came to hear him and his Constant Carolers Of The Lord. He said he laid his hand upon the seven seals every Sunday morning and whether they were about to break he couldn't say but he was ready to preach to any who would pray with him, always leaving the doors sprung wide to the world if it wanted to pass in and hear him out. He said he often stood in the doorway facing across the concession road, facing the twisting branch of the Saugeen that ran to the east side of the trailer park bounded by woods on one side and the field of wrecked cars on the other, a wrecking field owned by Isaac Shave, whose family had been pig farmers, and Lute said he talked to the land, he said he liked to get right down on his hands and knees and whisper to the land, which he said with a wide smile that he had a great lust for, and he wanted me to know that he had a great lust and believed each of his sermons that he delivered on Sunday mornings was a direct communiqué through him from what he called the Mother Ship of The Lord of Light, and I said, "You don't say," and I just sat down on the porch, worn out from everything, and let him settle his eyes on me, taking a gentleness and a blessing where I could, I suppose, as he went on and on like he was happily in the funnel of his own thoughts, the way Evol had always been before he went out turkey hunting, going on to say something to me about how the dead never died and how something I'd never heard of called the Starbelt of The Cosmic Megatron contained us all. I sat there staring at him and into a whiskey glass full of whiskey, but I didn't drink it, and I wasn't weeping or sobbing but tears were just flooding out of my eyes, tears I took no heed of, and neither did he, acting as if he wasn't a complete stranger but as if he'd been coming by to sit on my porch every day to listen to me singing low soothing words to myself, singing a mournful *Rock-a-bye baby in the tree top when the wind blows the cradle will rock* until I did start to sob because I couldn't believe what I knew was true and what I had to believe, that Loanne, after all the pain from the death of Evol, was actually dead and gone, and I therefore said

"Why do we go on believing what we know can't be true?"

"Like?" he said, angling forward on the edge of his chair.

"Like life everlasting is supposed to lie in God."

"It does for sure," he said, and I said

"God don't take no prisoners."

He fastened a look on me for a long time, like he was looking at a bird or a snake slowly come out of its shell, and I could see that behind the blessing of his yellowish eye there was something raw, some mulish rigor that was ready to be riled up inside him, already festering, but he suddenly stood up and smiled and said

"No time like the present for what's got to be done," and he left before I could ask him

"What do you got to get done?"

He went clomping down the gravel walk, revving up his truck like some left over thing was nagging on his mind, *rum, rum, rum,* and then I was alone, wondering why I'd let him, a complete stranger, stay there so long, and yet as soon as he was gone I missed him, that mulish thing, but he was gone, as was only right, leaving me sitting there like stale water in a jar with all of Loanne's loose and lacy things spread around me, and this swole my heart so much in my throat that I was about to choke, so I washed the swelling down with whiskey and wished on the name of my daddy, Wishbone Tull, and it was Tull because he

had cut the Tullamore down to Tull, so I wished that
the dying, unless they were intending to come back,
would take their belongings with them but of course in
my heart I didn't want any glimpse of Loanne in my
life to be gone, so I stayed there hardly moving like my
blood was standing still, smelling the rancid sweet
smell of a child's heated milk lingering like it was
glued to the air, staring at the swirl of bloody sheets,
listening to flies skitter and dance on the window glass,
always, hour after hour the buzzing of flies, the same
drowsing drone that three days later was in the air on
the morning of her funeral, the heat shimmering up out
of the bald ground all around us at the grave, and the
wasps clouding in the air, too, tasting and teasing
themselves on the lilac sweetness in the wind, slumber
sweetness of lilac and magnolia, the soft magnolia
cheeks of the minister who was telling us my child's
sweet soul had escaped to hatch again in the hatchery
mind of God, a sweetness of glory in the air and decay
in the earth that was drawing the scavenger wasps to
suck as though all our dead were always only decaying
fruit spilled to the ground, the dead once they were
really dead being only a pulp for feeding wasps, and so
I was glad when her box was shut tight, shut against

the light, against the air, against the scavengers, shut
and screwed down against the soil, against all seepage,
shut and gone though quickly a time came when I
thought she'd never truly gone, that the woman who'd
eased through the silvering into the room beside me
when my baby died wasn't me at all but was actually
my little girl when she was grown up, my little Loanne
standing somewhere down the line in time watching
me watch her die so she could judge whether she could
have trusted me to look after her. That's how I knew in
my marrow bones that she was still alive, lost to my
sight but close by me even after the burial because I
could feel her, feel her presence like the pulse of silence
in an empty church as I shifted her dolls around from
pillow to pillow, because she was there like love enclos-
ing a hollow, which is maybe what death is, love's hollow, but seeds will fall and gather in a hollow, so as the
days went by I just let the wind carry whatever seeds
were on the air, because I knew soon enough some
seeds'll rise up like the dead are supposed to rise up
out of their own seed boxes, since the dead are winter
flowers, at least that's what my momma always called
the dead, a world of winter immortelles we can only
see and talk to when they freeze on the window panes

the way frost on glass freezes and becomes flowers that look like the immortelles we used to press between sheets of glass, and so I have always loved clear glass because that's how Evol and me most of the time talked to each other, like glass, like there was nothing that stood between what we were trying to say to each other, which was not at all how it became with me and Lute, because with Lute he was always blurting out strange words full of forked talk, furious, like

"The locust feeds off the fruit of the fat land while the Lord abides and broods in the gravel stones that lie beneath, and all else is evil,"

so I said, "Lute, it's time to talk plain talk," but he closed his eyes and slumped and sat back and said nothing and a man who says nothing when something is necessary to be said is worse and maybe more dangerous than a liar, so I got into my stomping frame of mind and went out, stomping up and down the stairs of the stoop, and started lifting sheets of glass from the cardboard cartons stacked on the back of his truck. I never asked if I could take the glass, but he couldn't miss what I was doing and every other afternoon after that, after he drove up the lane and parked his truck, he came in and sniffed the air and then he put his nose against the inside of the screen in the door and watched. There was always freshly cut big panes of glass sitting out there between corrugated sheets of cardboard, like it was an unspoken gift that he was too shy to come right out and give me. Nothing was ever said, not about the glass, not about all the shapes and sizes, and he kept coming, keeping hold of a sullen quiet, except for his tremendous tendency to snatch some self-made saying out of his mind, because he had a whole cluster of preaching and pamphlet talk about what he called the Chimes of the Times and Tubular Bells of Atmospherica and he liked to say how these bells were cosmic filters for the Bread of God and it was the Bread of God that was in all stones, and he loved to talk about gravel, the gravel my daddy cursed, which Lute always carried fistfuls of in his pockets, so he said

"If the Lord is not the stone in your heart He's a stone in your shoe,"

and he'd rattle on, talking like that for ten minutes, talking about how the end and the rapture were near, how the great laying waste of the earth was almost upon us, but I also knew he was trying to figure out how to wheedle up on me without whingeing and snuffling like most men do, because I could smell a hunger he had in him, the heat, hardly holding his hands off me, and one day he said

"How come you were all alone with your girl when she died?"

and I said, scraping down fresh-pulled carrots for a stew

"Because Evol was gone."

"Who's Evol?"

"Loanne's daddy."

"Your husband's dead then?"

"He wasn't my husband, he was her daddy."

"You loved him?"

"Sure I love him, how could he be my lover if I didn't love him?"

"Easy," he said, "you could be my lover and not love me, except I'd want you to love me like you say you loved him."

"Didn't do me an inch of good, loving him."

"Why's that?"

"Killed himself. For a crime he didn't do except he did other crimes. He promised he'd live with me for all of my life and he didn't keep his promise and I hold that against him more than his killing himself. A broken promise is close cousin to an outright lie."

He was squinting at me like his eyelids had gone slack, which I could tell he thought was sly, and sexy, and it was, but that only left me wondering about how true the plumb-line of a come-by-chance preacher was, a preacher who sometimes seemed to be sniffing and poking around the edges of the house like it was the scene of a crime, nosing and sniffing in just the same way they say a criminal always comes back to see the crime he's done or the blood he's let, except Lute was no criminal, not that I knew of, but he was, so he said again, a fierce entrepreneur for the future and a preacher in the Shadow of God, calling himself a Polestar of the First Water for God, preacher Lute with his pale, pale eyes just like my father's eyes that seemed to lose all their yellow in the sunshine and turned to mercury, a darktime lustre in the daylight, staring, with a dull sour heat simmering in him, tamped down and staring but also talking more and more to me about harvesting the land, about raising up the gravel out of the great underground gravel beds, all the while rubbing the sharp knuckles of one hand into the palm of his other, working his ropey arms that were all sinew, and I had to admit that he was a good-looking man the more I looked at him, a man who wore every day a black high-

crowned stetson and a black and green plaid wind-
breaker like it was the tartan sign of some clan, though
he said his name came from somewhere I never heard
of, "No place on any map I ever saw." Luther Alm,
Lute, the son of Avery Alm, Lute the Map Man, that's
how I called him, because more and more he took to
talking about surveying and maps and unrolling these
wide government charts on the kitchen table, drawing
his own red lines on them, maps that already had deli-
cate wispy tracings like layers and layers of mud had
dried there, and he also had little prophesy pamphlets
and bible preaching tracts in his pockets, so that leaning over the maps, the yellow all lit up in his eyes, he'd
explain that there were places out across the world
where God had put His foot down, God had taken His
stand and His stand was out there in the electro-mag-
netic fields, that's what Lute called them, electro-mag-
netic fields where God had left His own individual
burn marks in the earth, burn marks in those places
that no one could explain, a sign of His stealthy presence and the promise of the burning to come, His
scorched earth, and Lute would hunker down talking
with this sorrowful rage about hell as the endhole of
our rancorous earth, the endhole where the sun set,

shrivelled, and never rose to shine again, getting himself more and more flushed as he suddenly stroked the back of my head, my hair, a quick hand, and it was like being brushed by a bird's wing, a night owl, which I didn't deflect or bristle at because I could also see that I was acting more and more forward and flirtatious to him, easing out of my own aloneness and logy feeling and pain by lingering there and listening to him. So he was off his hunkers and up on his own two feet day after day filling all the silence of the house with words, just the opposite to Evol who had the gift for a rush of words but also could just park his tongue and sit and sit, but Lute, he'd break out like a flushed animal, talking at me about magnetic fields and the foot prints of God while I figured some other beady thought had to be banging around between his eyes, something he hadn't come clean about, which made me want to flat out needle and provoke him, turning me more brazen about going out to his truck that was sitting there like he'd stalled a thought and I just took down glass sheets of all sizes, laying them out into hop-scotch squares in the garden plot behind the house but he didn't say a word about that. Not even the syllable of a word. And every day there were always more sheets of glass on the truck and he'd sit in the shutter-light from the kitchen window and slowly he drew his sleeve across the oil cloth on the kitchen table and squinted into the slits of light like he was looking a long long way into the future, looking for old stories to come true in the future, and sometimes he'd rest his hands on my hips so that I had to hold still before him, like the pause between us was a pause in the clock, or maybe the clock was running down but I couldn't be sure about that unless I went ahead and found out, knowing, like my momma said, "That even a run-down clock has got to be right twice a day." Then, early one morning when the long grass was still speckled with dew-light he showed up and the whole yard lay there sheeted with panes of glass fixed to the box frames I'd made and set in the earth from lengths of leftover aluminum siding trim, the glass shining like mirrors in the slanting morning sun with hundreds and hundreds of tiny green-white shoots salting the earth underneath, the black soil looking like it was stormed full of seed suddenly growing under the glass and he said

"God helps those who help themselves and you sure helped yourself."

I heard a fly skittering against the window, cracking its brains up against what it couldn't see the compass of or ever understand but still it was doing its dance till it fell down, and standing there I could feel the buzz in Lute's blood, hankering after me more and more every day as the hours eased toward dusk when there always seems to be that stillness that has no shadow, the hour when I get roused to the need to lie down like I used to lie down under Evol, the hour when I always walked the land or broke loose in my mind with Evol, wanting to feel that pain that gets so swollen with pleasure that I can hardly bear it, wrenching with a light that runs like spilt water through my veins and I sometimes have wondered if that isn't what Evol found for himself, the whole tonload of light that must have exploded behind his eyes, wanting to die into the seed of light like I wanted to die in Evol's arms, like Lute said he hoped to die and go to heaven in mine, calling himself my Lute, "I am your Lute," he said, but he only said that so forthrightly because he knew I wasn't his, not yet, not by a long shot, as he angled his words back and forth in the air between us like a string-game of cat's cradle, so that when we drove out one night to the Mortlake Roadside Bar and Dance Hall, a joint way beyond anywhere I usually went, a bar on the road to Kincardine that had a huge belt buckle mounted overhead on the roof in the sky in neon lights that looked like rhinestones flashing as the music blared into the parking lot, he took me by the hand, a courtly hand as we threaded our way through the truckers who were all dressed and got up real smart in their square-toed shitkickers, their long wallets jammed in their back pockets hooked to their belts by shiny nickel chains, and he shied away from the dance floor where everyone was twirling together, so proper and so polite in a nice lock-step like the line dancing they'd learned on country television shows, and he turned us into the lowly lit bar where everything was chrome and clip-on with a girl wearing something skimpy and strapless who had a tattoo of Jesus on her shoulder blade, and she was playing pool at the pool table up front, and on the square center stage platform behind the bar a big sign that said THE FAT LADY DON'T SING HERE, SHE SHAKES because the girl stripper was a great big fat girl with her skin in rolls and bloated-looking arms and possum eyes and puckered thighs that were all pudgy and great hanging breasts that lolled to the side with big wide nipples and all I could think of was magnolias, that or white fat pork rind, sweet white rind on the edge of being rancid before you could eat it, while the fat girl kind of flounced and bounced and the men stood there silent and slack-jawed or cheering as she smiled stupidly, saying over and over again into the microphone, "The fat lady don't sing here," and Lute got fitful and snarky right away when we sat down, like he'd planned it that way, looking mean rather than dangerous, chewing on his lower lip and not even watching the fat girl or the other mingy girls with angel dust in their eyes dancing on top of the bar naked, telling the men to "fold your money, boys, fold your money," and I turned to puzzling on how they could squat and snatch up folded money with themselves, which twisted my mind, so I sat there trying to tense myself on the stool and figure out how a woman could get herself to grip that way, or want to, and I said

"How come a sanctifier like you wants to hang out with me in this pighole?" and still sullen for no good reason he says, "I deride the devil, I don't deny him,"

having a real pinched and petty look in his eyes, inward and sorry for himself, more and more sour, suddenly saying

"Sometimes you make me feel like next to nothing," and I said

"You're not next to nothing, you're next to me,"

but he didn't laugh, he scowled, so I told him
what my momma had told me when I was a girl, how

"There was a man who cried because he had no
shoes until he met a man who had no feet," and that
brought him up so short in his chair that he said, alert
and abrupt,

"How long ago'd Evol die?" and I said

"If he'd lived till Saturday he'd be dead a year."

Lute's grin at that was more like he'd been gutted than he was having a good time because he had no
gift at all for making light of dying, so we slowly eased
up on each other and told stories and talked all kinds of
tattle on ourselves about when we were kids until we
laughed and it turned out that he had a big boomy
laugh, not one of those up-your-nose laughs, a boomy
laugh which I liked, and then we left the bar and
danced for an hour under the big slow spinning
exhaust fans in the ceiling, two-stepping like we'd been
born to it under the fans that didn't suck up any of the
smoke but just stirred it around, and again we laughed
at ourselves as we danced, not laughing to each other's

face but over each other's shoulder, like laughing out the window in the room of somebody you just met, and when we got home to the house and parked in the lane he hunched over the wheel, peering into the darkness beyond the big angora white dice dangling from his rear view mirror, looking deep into the dark humps of the hills under the moonlight, the whole farm hump-backed, and he said

"You give off too much mourning, you got the rank smell of mourning on you, you're gonna be a god-damn mourning dove."

"I am, am I?"

"Yes you are."

"Well I do what I do."

I could tell he wanted to say something quick-tongued and acid and hurtful but instead he sat like he was clenching his brain, enclosed in his own stillness and taking deep breaths, stroking his nose, stroking the tip, until he said

"Well, goodnight to you."

"Tomorrow will take care of itself," I said, "and you take care of yourself," trying to ease us out of whatever the hurt was that he was holding onto and I could see that he was a man who held onto his hurts, who harbored his hurts and liked to clamp onto them, sitting up poker-straight and aloof, feeling so slighted that he'd gone and got himself huffy and reedy in his voice and near ready to strike, and I was just about to touch him like a child and let him nestle on me when he said goodnight again, still full of pride, saying, "I'm too old to take care of myself, and maybe you've known a jerk-off or two in your day but I ain't one, and anyway, the Lord will take care of me," so I got out saying I didn't mean to say nothing about jerking off and he backed slowly down the lane in the dark, leaving me to go in to a troubled sleep where I kept hearing the sound of bare feet walking up above.

"Keep your feet dry, and your powder," but when I opened my eyes, there was no space up above, there was only the slope of the ceiling and the angle of shadows. I lay awake all night, watching the slow shift of the angles, the light. I kept thinking of carousel horses and trying to hum a tune but my throat was tight and dry. I watched the first glimpse of dawn light on my own bare feet uncovered at the end of the bed. Like the light was coming through the skin between the bones, pink and almost flossy. Foolish light, because it seemed so peaceful. A child's light, the clammy dampness of dawn like my child's cold sweat on my bare body. Then, as the morning haze burned away, I got up and dressed and went for a walk outside the house. I could see, like I was seeing the house for the first time in a long while, that it was suffering all the warps that came from my having neglected it, leaving it unpainted with some shingles loose, and I saw there were bobolinks circling and looping, and finally they stooped down and set to walking on Lute's glass sheets laid out all over the yard, pecking at the shoots they could see but couldn't get through to, and I thought that was a damned sight funny, those birds trying to step through the glass, and when Lute drove up I said

"The birds are prancing on your glass."

He said, "The mice are shitting on the poison," making me know that he'd been brooding all night and that he still had a hickey on his heart and a bone to pick, and that he was a real windsucker who didn't think birds tap dancing on his glass was funny at all. Without a warning word, like he was setting out to walk a solid mile, he started tromping over the glass, trudging sheet by sheet, grim and head down, crashing and stomping his big yellow Greb work boots, and I came at him yelling and flapping my arms but he kept on till the field of glass was all broken. He stood there up to his ankles in mud and long blades of light and crushed seedlings that nosed up into the air, bloodless worms, the glass sticking up splintered and

"That was my glass," he yelled.

"Those're my seedlings."

"They're still yours, but what's mine was mine,"

and then with his bow-legged gait he strode down the laneway to the truck where he paused and laid his hand on the headlight and screwed up his face and hollered

"And the locust shall not nestle in my heart or rest upon the stone beds that are the seed of what is to be mine, for the bookkeeping of Bilan is a precise and meticulous process,"

which hauled me back on my heels, gawking, because I didn't know for the life of me what he was talking about, what with locusts and bookkeeping and stone seeds, and anyway he'd been keeping his bursts of testifying to next to nothing so I wasn't used to it. As he got up into his cab and drove off churning dust down the laneway, I thought, "He's sly. He is damn well sly," because he had to mean something beyond what he was saying. All that Bilan the Bookkeeper gabble. On the following day, and all the days after through a run of flash thunderstorms and cloudbursts, the seedlings swole up into stems and the broken glass sank down into the swarming green creepers and crab grass. I had a dream that all my family had congregated under the creepers and broken glass. By the end of the week Lute came back with some six foot lengths of white plastic picket fencing which he proceeded to set up around the yard, driving home plastic stakes with the claw-hammer he always carried on his thigh, the handle slipped through a loop sewn to his black jeans, and he said

"Now you got yourself a nice little lady-like patch of garden with a picket fence, you should put sunflowers in there,"

and he put his arm around my shoulder and hugged me, and said he was sorry, and I honestly could say that not too many a man had ever said he was sorry to me, so we went into the parlor, both of us wary about saying any kind of wrong words because wrong words is what always warps the air between people, like my momma and daddy lived their lives in a warp, though they loved each other for sure, at least I believed it, and some of what we believe has got to be true, so I laughed and I said that if he didn't want to celebrate my glass garden and picket fence with some whiskey then I did. He looked kind of crossways at me when I laughed, but he answered that whichever way the world went for us this day, he was willing to go, too. "You don't have to say you're sorry," I said, so he said he was sorry again. I laughed and poured him a whiskey. He stared into the glass like he was looking through a hole, so I knew right away that he was a man afraid of ever losing control, of ever giving an inch of himself away, especially after he swallowed the drink down whole and sighed, a look in his yellow eyes as if he'd just slit his wrists. He poured himself another drink.

"Some of us carry a warning halo around us," he said.

"I don't see no light when I look in the mirror," I said, but he said

"You got a halo about you anyway. The children of Light are raised up from the children of Darkness, and I saw right away you wear a halo."

"I do?"

"Yes you do."

"That's a nice thing for you to say."

"It means you're not going to die, not now."

"I'm not afraid of dying," I said, because even if death is a sore spot on my mind, and who could blame me with the burden of burials I've been through, I never thought about dying, never saw my own bones crossed in the air.

"What do you think we do when we die?"

"We all come back," I said.

"In the rapture," he said.

"I don't know about rapture," I said, "but I sure as hell know I wouldn't like to come back in any rapture as a cow, because cows must have done something very bad to be like they are, their eyes are so dumb. They just stand there, so it must be terrible being trapped inside a cow, hearing yourself talk inside a cow. No sir, what I'd like to be is water, rainwater with the scent of magnolia that disappears on someone's face in the night, except water always leaves its mark, a stain, to mark where it's been, and over the years a drop of water must leave a hundred million stains," and Lute, looking at me like he was looking at a lunatic, reached out and took hold of my wrist and said

"I don't want to ever disappear, ever," hunching up and suddenly morose. "No, I don't intend to disappear," and he chugged a mouthful of whiskey straight from the bottle. "No," he said, "because I know there's a ladder on which there are angels like children, and I've seen the stones that He said are the seed that shall be as nations, the children who are the heritage of the Lord, and the fruit of the womb is His reward. Psalm 127." I felt then and there that he'd seen his bones crossed in the air at least once, that there was a flayed spot in him, the way when you go pet a dog and it shies its head away and you know it's been beaten. He said

"Don't you ever see anything in the sky?" And I said

"Sure, sometimes I make my mind the sky."

"I been scared," he said. "But it's okay, because I get a grip on myself when I get scared by lying down and counting numbers, like some people count sheep to put themselves to sleep, except I count to keep calm, I love counting, it calms me, because when things go belly-up you've got to be calm and I can tell you, once one night I counted to over ten thousand because I've been belly-up but I ain't no fish,"

and since I was standing behind him in the shuttered light, he just sank back into my arms and rested there, his head between my breasts like he was dozing, but keeping his eyes open, staring like all the walls in the room had fallen down and he was lost somewhere in that pocket of silence between us, leaving me to try and tally the weight of what had passed between us since the afternoon of the broken glass, and then I heard as crisp as dead leaves crushed in your hand, Evol talking whisper talk, except he wasn't talking to me, and so I kept still behind Lute and waited to make sure if it was Evol, and then I yelled, "Talk to me, why aren't you talking to me?" near scaring Lute to death, so that he leapt and whirled around looking like he'd seen the ghost of himself in a mirror, and I felt all the blood in my head banging as I tried to hear again what I'd heard of Evol's voice, but I couldn't hear anything, not a word, no word at all, meaning maybe it was only me inside my head, my own wishful words, with Lute clutching at me, his hands on my breasts, pressing my breasts against his face and suddenly I could smell him, he had the smell of wild flower leaves and peat moss in his skin, making me want the heat of his mouth on my throat so that the two of us before we knew it were shucking our clothes and slipping down to the floor under the overhead wagonwheel lamp with two of the

candlebulbs burned out, feeling the pain to my own
backbone on the floor, jarred against the floor from his
coming down on me, hacking for air till the ache like a
brush-burn inside my skin took hold between my legs
and up into my throat so I felt I was wrenching open
and apart just like when I gave birth to Loanne, the
same cry of pain that was like someone else's pleasure
echoing out of me, and him hollering too, except this
time it was like my soul escaping out of my body, it
leapt right out between my legs like it was never coming back when I suddenly heard Evol whispering again
inside my head with Lute slumped on top of me and
breathing in my ear like he was about to die and I tried
to say I wanted my soul to come back inside me but
Evol was talking so low I could hardly hear him though
I could feel the tremor of his voice and then there was a
silence, and then Loanne was talking back to him,
quiet, confiding, as if I wasn't there, and I wasn't
because they weren't talking to me, they were talking
to each other, somewhere in a place beyond where my
words were, out in some loneliness, maybe along with
the loons, which sent an awful ache through my whole
body and I let out this moan and Lute thought it was
the after-pleasure of what we'd done and it was but in

a way he'd never know or understand so I kissed his cheek with just the brush of a kiss to thank him for the two voices being born again to me with their words so hushed I could hardly make them out, words that went on for a long time till I fell asleep with Lute already sleeping the sleep of the dead in my arms, listening to loons laughing the devil's laugh.

CHAPTER THREE

WHERE ME AND MOMMA ARE from, it's what Evol called daughter-fondling country, because when you walk into a room you seldom find more than two fingers of forehead on anyone, which does not mean that their brains are gone, or even that they are stupid, but they are concentrated, which can often pass for being stupid. And you don't ever want to make the mistake of thinking that a concentrated man is stupid, because he'll have you for breakfast. He'll have you before breakfast. He'll have you in his

71

sleep. And the most concentrated of concentrated men are men of the Lord, but they got a hard place in their souls that would make you wince. There's a mean thing in men of the Lord. So I kept waiting for the meanness in Lute. Lord knows, he had all the sanctifying down pat, the way he could soothe the snake in your heart, with his hands, with words. He'd sometimes hum when we were making love and I'd ease into a low humming too and one night I heard Evol humming with us in a harmony and I began to laugh but Lute's humming right away hardened into a hurt and then when he'd made it clear how hurt he was, he got into a forgiving tone of sanctimony, but I had already learned his kind of forgiveness was like a scab, a scab that's supposed to be a sign of healing while what's under a scab is pus, a wound waiting to be picked and opened and what's mean about men of the Lord is that they like to open up wounds. Scab pickers. There's stone pickers and scab pickers, and by and large that's who settled this land that we are on, people who kept picking stones like they were dead eggs out of the earth so that the earth could come from fallow into seed, and then there were those who dreamed of hatching themselves out of life by dying, by leaping into the arms of the Lord. "Lepping," my momma called it. "Lepping for the Lord," and she wasn't given to mulling and mewling around in her mind and questioning the things she believed, so she found it hard to believe that a farmer who was rooted to the earth could ever kill for no good reason and she saw no good reason for hanging yourself unless it was for the Lord, so if a snowbound farmer had hung himself in the dead of winter, she'd screw up her tiny eyes in her sockets and say, "Who do you think the demon is in you, I ask you that?" and Evol, who had a liking for momma though she wasn't so quick to cotton onto him, said, " The demon has you in hand, whoever he is, when you kill someone," and she said

"But Jesus killed himself. He came to die and he knew he was going to die and got himself killed and the only bad thing is that there are folks who've been blamed for killing Jesus when Jesus killed himself and no one would have killed him if he hadn't of wanted to die, so as far as I can figure, dying is what he stood for, saying if he died we'd all live, but to live like he wanted us to live we've all got to die before we live."

Evol had stared at her hard and long and then said, "I'd hate to know what you think about love."

"I don't think about love," she said, "but I do love when I can."

Nobody said a word except Evol, who was so intense that he could stand inside the rain when it rained, standing somewhere deeper than solitude, with his eyes having forgotten how to be young, and he said, "There's bits and pieces of love lying out there littered all around us. That's how you know there's been love. It's in the junk," and I wanted to laugh because I couldn't imagine Isaac Shave's scrap yard of old cars and junk being any kind of love heap, but Evol was busy cornering his thought, and he started talking about all that's left behind by us, like they were clues, he said, "All the clues to love, the breakage and junk, the bits and spillage from tinkering, and broken handles and torn up drainage tiles and rusted sickles and hammer-heads and pump-plungers and gaskets and old license plates with magic numbers and camshafts and split axles and split foundation stones and all the tumbled split-rail fencing and broken light bulbs in broken lamps, all the leftovers lying in the ragweed, leftovers that do not lie," he said, "but only tell a truth about how someone together with someone else tried to make their lives come alive, tried to make their being

alive something more than pain and the closeness of
death, so the things that they left behind, things that
can be broken and busted and half-buried, are still
never got rid of, not forever, and they are all we have
and all we need to tell us, no matter how worn out and
bruised they are, how hard some folks tried to move
fallow land into the light, tried to carry the tangled
dark earth into the arms of someone else who had the
same dumb yearning and this is what we see in a worn
handle, all their words worn down to a handle-grip,
lost," and momma, listening to him, was clutching the
mail-order gold cross she wore on a chain around her
neck, a cross with a magnifying bead of glass at the
crux which let you read the whole of the Lord's Prayer
if you squinted up close. "Their words are lost but not
the wood," Evol said, "the shine of the wood doesn't
get lost, and the smoothness of the handle is lying out
there somewhere to show that love was once alive in
this hard place because stubble and gravel stones are
not all there is, not by a long shot, not by the Book, not
by malice, not by gum, not by Jesus, but two-by-two,"

and Evol was up on his feet doing a little step
dance which was not surprising because he did love to
dance, saying, whispering, "Two people tending to

each other, trying to tamp each other down when there's terror, and maybe they find a charred old timber and plane and square it to a window sill so that they can sit on either side of the sill and stare into each other's face and see right there, the way we do, what they just rescued, which is what I'd want to say about love for now, which is what I want to say to the woman I love, here, safe in the darkness, unscarred against the wall."

"What about that jar?" Momma said, hardly giving a moment's pause to what he'd said as he stood staring at me while I stared back because I'd never heard so many words in a row out of him.

"What jar?"

"The jar that was buried out back," and she was talking about a big old one-gallon glass jar that had been buried by someone, but only up to the top of the silver shining lid, so that when the sun was out good and strong, the lid shone, a circle of light at the roots of the long grass, and we all saw it at the same time one day while we were out walking, right by the edge of the boundary line, as if that's exactly how we were supposed to find it by whoever had set the jar down in the earth, because if the jar had been buried only two inches deeper it would never have been found, so the finding was intended like nearly everything in life is intended and has its signification, and it was dug up and we held it at arms length so that we could see in there, like a taunt or challenge, a child. A small tiny child. Born before term and entombed in glass. All withered and a pink leathery color and squeezed down into a glass jar, like someone had not only birthed and then got rid of the child but couldn't bear to get rid of it forever, couldn't bear to put it truly back in the earth to rot and be lost and forgotten and so had encased it in the glass jar, leaving it sitting in there like a ship in a bottle. Staring for who knows how long into the darkness of the earth until one afternoon we dug it up and momma howled and roared at the sight of it, or more exactly him, because it was a him, his little dark nub pointed straight at us, poised, and Evol, he turned right around on his heel and went back to the house and got his turkey gun and then set the jar on a fence post, the shrivelled tight body huddled, the head flooded by light, and he aimed at it up close and fired straight into the face and blew the jar and the boy child all to pieces, the glass exploding.

"What about what was in the jar?" my mother said again, but Evol only smiled, so she said in the way she was used to baiting daddy, "You killed it, you shot that child into nowhere," and Evol said

"I didn't kill it."

"Yes you did."

"It was already killed. By its mother, whoever she was."

"But you shot it away so there was nothing left."

"I shot it away so its ghost could walk, and its ghost is still with us, and walking among us as the reminder of what was once a time of love between two people, and now the ghost is alive and making tracks in my mind if not in yours."

And it was that night in bed that Evol and I made love to make Loanne because Evol said he could feel the ghost of that child walking up and down his back while he was up and down on me, and we tried so hard that the seed took and when the month came that I didn't bleed, that was the month Evol said that he had quit hearing the footsteps of the child, and so he said something was alive out of something that was evil, making Loanne truly a love child, which led to a happiness that was unlooked for, although what's unlooked for usually ends up staring you straight in the eye in the dark. But this love child was a light like the Lord is supposed to be to us, a lightening of feeling among us, even with daddy who usually took a scunner to any man who stood in his doorway let alone a man who was a lover to me, and momma, she was just plain puckered up with suspicion, believing that no man meant any woman any good, which is what she'd got from her momma and had passed on down to me, though it was no different from what the young dollies she saw on TV were saying, "As if they're telling me something I don't know, except they say it nastier," she said, but then she went ahead and behaved as if what she knew to be true didn't matter because she took Evol into the house, took him in like he was a son, a son who was about to bestow a son on her out of me. Wishbone Tull my daddy had never made it a secret that no matter how many times he said he loved me, he'd have loved a son more, and it was this yearning after more and then more that got to my momma and daddy, that seemed to taunt them with all the disappointments they'd had in their life and the dreams they'd lost, so that what they shared was a rancor of the heart that wasn't anybody's fault in particular, but it was there between them, always, because they couldn't let go of each other, they couldn't think of anywhere else to be, not really, so any tenderness or touching between them was like getting prickly heat, especially after he lost his left arm, like the wishbone had been broken and he'd come up short, so touching between them was nearly always too uncomfortable, too wrapped up in what could have been, except when daddy got randy and blind drunk, and when he was like that there was no way to temper the rancor except to sit as still and silent as possible and the best way to do that was to cluster around and watch television. Sitting in the dark parlor watching television took away the temptation to talk eye-to-eye. It can take a long time to turn an hour around on the clock without talk, so momma and daddy could sit into the night letting the tube haze the room with light and if they said a word to each other, it was by way of the TV, always staring the TV straight in the eye, and that way they had fun, though they'd never say so, nagging away at the government, believing their lives had been stolen from them by what they called "shit-faces" and "shit-heels" from the city, and daddy would pound his one fist on the chair, glaring, taking whatever he saw on television as a direct insult, but he surprised us all and slipped out of his shoes with Evol, I guess because Evol had a natural gift for keeping his mouth shut, which daddy took as a sign of respect, saying one night

"I like a man who says nothing knowing he has nothing to say." The only thing that troubled daddy was that Evol was not of our prayer persuasion. He told daddy not to worry about that and when daddy said, "Why not?" he said because he came from a long line of freethinking footloose shoemakers and horse traders, horsemen who came from way back before the famine boats and the cholera time when everybody had come out from the old country, and he was a Dewan, which he said was an old name that his father told him had just appeared out of nowhere

and daddy opened and closed his fist and opened it again because he liked to think of himself as a stern man but an open man of no malice. Evol told him about his father, a man, he said, who knew how to stand in the middle of things and not lose his balance, a man who had once owned a white horse, back when the two prayer persuasions had begun talking with some ease to each other, even if, in the underswell of real feeling, they still stood apart, skewing each other. Skewed or not, they knew there couldn't be a parade in town without a white horse

"So my father," Evol said, "he offered to lend them his white horse, and they borrowed the horse, except right in the middle of the parade, it up and slumped down and died of a heart attack, rolling over and nearly crushing King Billy, who was the County Clerk, a man called Bigelow. And my father, he said the horse, being Catholic and feeling betrayed, had died of a broken heart and so he would accept no money but asked only that his beloved white horse be given a proper burial in a good plot of ground, which he left up to them. And they buried the horse, but what they didn't say to him or anybody else is that they hauled the horse in the middle of the night to the Catholic graveyard of The True Cross and buried him there, leaving the four hoofs sticking up above ground, unnoticed in the summer grass, but they were found out in the winter when high winds blew the snow clean off the mound. There were the four hoofs sticking up like markers for the prowling devil, sticking up in consecrated ground, so the burying party was ordered by everyone to get the white horse out of its grave before some serious trouble broke out but getting the horse up was a problem because the ground was frozen solid and since no one would let them wait till the spring, they went in and drilled four holes, one by each hoof, and dropped in sticks of dynamite like candles and blew that horse to nowhere, right out of the ground, sacred as it was," and Daddy kept clapping his hands, saying, "Jesus Christ, that was the Great Getting-up Day for that damned horse, that was the Great Getting-up Day."

He laughed and laughed. I'd seldom seen him laugh so hard, and so I was thankful to Evol, and daddy was too in a strange way, not just because of the horse story but because Evol never did make the mistake of talking about anything close to daddy's contention bone. Daddy didn't brook contention, and he did have what he took to be his dignity. Maybe he had so strong a sense of his own dignity to protect because he was so disappointed, but it was also a dignity he himself derided, as if derision was one of the few freedoms he still had. But no one could cross him. He was the last word in his own house. Still, Evol made him laugh, and he'd also made me pregnant, so there was laughter and happiness loose in the house as I moved into the last months of what my momma still liked to call my confinement though I was strong as a horse and wasn't confined at all. I did feel cocooned, but that's a different thing, and no sooner did I feel the comfort of that cocoon, never needing to look farther than the far field, than out of nowhere came a travelling country carnival setting up for a week on the Base Line road, right where the old Carlson family lime kilns had been, on what was known as Kiln Korner, bringing in a small ferris wheel and a carousel and all kinds of pitch-and-toss games, as well as two freaks for the Freak Show. I went along with everybody since daddy, to all our surprise, said we should go. "We should all go and have a blistering good time." So we went at dusk one Wednesday night. And it was beautiful, walking down the concession road between the split-rail fences, seeing the small pretty white ferris wheel against the flaring red in the spring sky, the little lights on the wheel rolling, and Evol, laughing, sang out

> *Ezekial saw a wheel a-rolling,*
> *way in the middle of the air,*
> *a wheel within a wheel a-rolling,*
> *and the little wheel run by Faith*
> *and the big wheel run by the grace of God*

and we could hear the rinky-tinky music of the carousel from a long way off, and I had the feeling we were truly going back into momma's girlhood because only the week before she had suddenly stopped seeing daddy's face in the sink water, she had stopped daydreaming that he was dead by drowning, and instead she had got up and scrubbed herself clean and washed her hair and braided it and talked about how she'd dressed in white when daddy had courted her. Her white ruffled dress was still in a box in their closet. And on the day the carnival arrived she was all ready with her white dress, but then she didn't wear it, because she couldn't button it up the back. There were all kinds of farmers at the carnival, and folks from Crudup's trailer park playing games like Fishing Hole, trolling with a tin pole in a water tank for number tags that'd give them a stuffed Snoopy dog, and some tried to knock down big wooden milk bottles by throwing a soft baseball, although everybody knew one of the bottles had a fistful of lead shot in the bottom so it would never fall down. What made the games even more-strange to us is that they were run by Indians. All my life, only Indians from a reservation way out by Penetanguishine ever ran carnivals and daddy said it was like playing with ghosts, "They look right through you," and momma said, "Yeah, but what makes it more peculiar is that their eyes are smoke. You look in their eyes and all you see is smoke. They ain't human like we are, they're human like somebody else." We all went into a tent that was the Temple Of The Exotic to see the two freaks, two brothers whose lizard skin was turning to stone. One had brown eyes. The other had a blue eye and a brown eye. They didn't look at anybody who looked at them, while the pitchman who was the boss said, "Thank your lucky stars, you don't have to live like this, turning to stone from the outside in." He tapped their shoulders with a riding crop. Their skin gave a deadfall sound. "Two brothers. Pity the mother, the fruit of her womb, about to be stone." Their skin looked like overlapping scales and scabs. "Two years at most to live, they'll die with hearts of stone." The brothers then sang a duet in high, reedy voices

> *Rock of ages cleft for me,*
> *Let me hide myself in Thee,*
> *Let the water and the blood*
> *From thy riven side which flowed*
> *Be of sin the double cure*

as a canvas curtain with a teepee afloat on ocean waves painted on it dropped in front of them. The lights went down. When we came out of the tent, daddy was whispering to momma

"What's gone is gone."

"I know that, I just wanted to wear my white dress again."

"You can do that but it don't change nothing because change of life is change of life."

"It's not fair," and I remembered momma saying that very same thing to me when I was a girl who'd just become a woman, the blood coming on one morning. I wasn't scared. I'd been waiting for it. I'd had to wait a little while, too, but then momma was upset because she'd not only married late, but she'd lost her cycle early, the year I got mine, and she'd thought that that was unfair and a taunt to her and ever since she'd been a little strange, like she thought I'd robbed her of something. Daddy had just shrugged and said, "Look it up in Leviticus, it's in the blood." We didn't know what he meant, except it was his way of accounting for the strangeness of women, and a few of the girls and women I knew did take strange, like the six Carlson sisters and their mother who all got their periods at the same time every month. "There's some kind of cuckoo clock in the blood," momma said. "I'd hate to find myself in a nunnery of Carlsons all going cuckoo at the same time." Momma and I laughed at that, but we didn't laugh at much together. She got more convinced that my coming to womanhood had stolen hers, like it was a sign that her life was over when mine was beginning, with her getting morose and moody, talking about sudden heat swells inside her body that were trying to suffocate her. She warned me not to make love when I was bleeding. "The child will get the portwine stain on his head," she said, "a sign you did it in the blood."

"Didn't you?" I said.

"Never," she said, and looked at me sideways.

On the night one of the Shave boys took me back into the woods, I looked at the blood on my thighs. I wasn't worried about blood and saw it in some of the strangest places, like Evol's turkey beards that he nailed to all the doors. They were like tongues, rusty colored tongues the color of my bleeding. And I called out to Evol who was sauntering along in the light of the carousel

"Evol."

"Yes."

"What're you doing?"

"Walking."

"To where?"

"Wherever you're going."

I sidestepped over to Evol away from my momma and daddy and took his arm.

"Didn't you hate having to look at those two?" I said.

"Nope."

"I hated it."

"I saw them freaks ten years ago, when I was a kid, when I was fourteen. Except they had a sister then, too."

"You mean they're not going to die?"

"Of course they're going to die. Nothing to be done about that, for none of us." He squeezed my arm and said, "So you better hold onto me while you can." The sun went down, and the loveliest thing to see in the dark was all the neighbormen and their wives on the carousel wheel of painted ponies, carrying their children and grandchildren in their laps, revolving in a rise and fall around and round and in and out of the light of bare bulbs strung above the ponies. Another line of lights was strung out over a path through the darkness to the gate to the ferris wheel, a high turning wheel in the night wind, turning to the scent of dew and new grass on the air

and it was the scent on the wind that clung to me the scent of dew on new grass in the night, and it stayed with me and kept me sane, or partly sane through the burials and the on-coming summer until late in July when Loanne was born.

Though the blooming summer heat of August was heavy and the sun stood bald in my eye and the cluster flies gummed up against my face and hair whenever I walked out, I walked out a lot because I was strong enough to cross the fields alone without Evol, who was working at the auto wrecking lot, carrying Loanne, stopping to hold her close to my face and inhale great deep breaths of her and how she smelled of dew and green apples and lilac bark. She put her tiny finger up to my lips all at once like she was stopping me from saying a word, not letting me say one word more out loud, though I only wanted to speak to her about my dead momma and daddy, and how she'd lost her grandfather and grandmother, a man and a woman who'd only ever be a small photograph stuck in her dresser mirror. They had died with him looking perky as he sat up straight in the ferris wheel chair with his one arm in the air, the two of them laughing like children. Looking back I said to Loanne, "Don't you worry, I'll never let anything like that happen to you," which, as it turned out, was the first lie I told her, so maybe Loanne was giving me a warning with that tip of her finger to my lower lip, a warning not to tell her lies, the finger of a babychild who seemed to be too wise, the wise child I'd given birth to, though that was a kind of lie in itself because I didn't give her anything if you consider that no woman really gives birth, since the child was there in me and I carried her and she took and fed from me and then leaped like one of momma's leppers, full of hope and trust into the air like it was the morning of the world, which is why I figure the morning air's fresh and so full of hope and trust, otherwise we'd kill ourselves, but the morning air can also fool you, because the shadows don't seem to fall, they rise in the morning, so that by noon nothing has any shadow at all though it's there, which is how it was for Emma Easley, a woman who sometimes seemed to cast no shadow, who lived with her husband Albert at Crudup's. It was like she'd slept in till noon but she was sudden with life in her belly at the same time as me, and she used to come around to the house and talk to me kindly and was always considerate of the little niceties, that's what she called them, the little niceties, as she grew so big over seven months that she got sway-backed and flat-footed and stared

happily stupid at me as she stood in my front door. But
with her, at last, there was nothing there, not a thing.
It was all air, no hope or trust on the morning wind.
Or maybe that's wrong. Maybe it's the other way
round, maybe all her hope and trust were inside her,
feeding on her like a child feeds, and it was the beat of
hope in her that she could feel, like wings, a buzzard's
wings feeding the pain that comes on like the latch
between your hips is cracking open. Though some doctor had said that he was dead sure he'd heard the
heartbeat, two months early she delivered herself of
nothing. She locked herself in her kitchen and cried,
"My belly is Nod country," and she tried to shoot herself in the head but missed and shot the canary in the
kitchen cage, which struck her as so damn useless and
typical of herself that she subsided into daylong giggling and smirking, wearing a bandana around her
head and sometimes slipping it down over her eyes,
trying to walk around blindfolded in her kitchen without banging into things but she only really lost the
handle on herself when she was oven-baking, and then
she would cover her face white with flour and begin to
hoot like a night owl *Hoo, hoo, hoo, hoo.* Otherwise, she
was pretty much under control, though she kept com-

ing around after Evol had gone to work to talk to me,
full of heartfelt and consoling sympathy for all the
pain of what she called, "Actually birthing a baby."
She was so full of sadness that sometimes I'd give her
an armload of flowers and tumble them into her lap
while she sat telling me about the pain, my pain, my
fear, and how it had all been and then she'd start
counting, quietly counting so that I'd join in with her,
breathing to the count, and then we'd start coming out
of the count and into the contractions, into a dry heav-
ing for air and it made me want to weep for such a sad
mortified woman who had become a twin to me, a
birthday sister, and for so long as Evol was not home,
working that month at laying tiles for drainage ditches,
and so long as Loanne was in another room sleeping
quietly, all Emma Easley could talk about over and
over was the thing I could hardly remember, the three
hours of lying splayed back with her feet in the stir-
rups, and she'd get this look in her eye like she was on
a high wild ride with no tight-rope in the long valley
of her own loneliness, and listening to her I could feel
the depth of pain that had come from my own child's
head bearing down against my tailbone, a pain deep
inside all my veins, so deep I couldn't hear my own

screaming, and I started, right there in the kitchen, to scream again, just like I'd done when Loanne had been born, and all our yelling woke the sleeping child who started to howl too like she was howling with us, and at the sound of the child, a horror crossed Emma Easley's face as she sat there knowing in her bones what the feel of nothing is, having taken a man's seed and given birth to absence, sitting there panic-stricken in the kitchen. She suddenly crumpled and fell into my arms, weeping, her head bent against my slack belly and full breasts and with the wetness of milk staining through my blouse, wetting her cheek, I had the strangest urge to nurse her, to cradle her and feed her, but it was a tenderness I had no right to risk, so she just rested her head in my lap, moaning quietly. Loanne had settled and was lying in her crib wide awake. I thought something must be wrong, because when I got up to look at her she was just lying there staring, staring like maybe she'd been struck dumb by the moving finger of God or her tongue had been stung by a bee. But there was nothing wrong. Not with her. Not with me.

"All they got out of me," Emma Easley said, "what with the enema and all, was shit." She stood up.

She stood very erect and brushed her hair away from
her eyes. I'd seen that stern melancholy look before in
my mother so many times on so many days. I had it in
me, too. Except it's more than melancholy. It's a kind
of contempt, a contempt that you cull out of disappointment, all the disappointments you nose around in
in your life till you feel like you're a junkyard dog.
Mocking and long-suffering contempt. Her contempt
was one way momma had kept from killing my daddy.
She didn't want to kill him. I'm sure she loved him at
least a little, but so much had gone awry and so much
had come up empty that sometimes when they sat
watching TV in the dark all I could feel was a melancholy, the same melancholy that was so deep in Emma
Easley, so deep in her limbs that her arms and legs
seemed to lengthen the more responsible she felt, the
more fault she took upon herself. She figured it was
her fault for believing that an air pocket in her belly
was a child, so therefore she was responsible for her
husband's shame and loathing. All this was in the way
she breathed. Quietly, measured. She measured all her
pain every moment of the day, and she measured her
steps, and every breath was measured, counted. I
could feel her measuring her breath as she walked out

of the room, out onto the porch, reaching her hand out into a light rain that had begun to fall, but no sooner had she gone partway down the lane than it began to pour, bringing a heavy chill on the wind, not like a winter chill, but the chill when you're bone-weary, when you're so tired you can feel wet leaves in your skin. As I watched her walk down the lane

it came to me that almost no woman I've known has ever talked about the pain of birth, it being a pain locked to the back of the mind, like men do with war, at least the men who've come back from war who live around here. They sit like old women in the Legion Hall. The older they get the lower their bellies sink and the higher their trousers come up to their chest, so that one old man I once saw was close to wearing his belt-buckle for a bow-tie, and I've been in there at night in the Hall playing darts, since daddy was a great darts player, licking the point of his dart, standing silent as silent could be in the narrow long smoke-filled hall, tense, always trying for a triple 20, and hitting the 1 altogether too many times, but never complaining. He never complained before other men. He swallowed his remorse and disappointment with himself whole, swallowed it down inside like you stuff a goose, but he was no goose. He was dangerous, he could have killed someone, though he was no soldier. He'd fallen between wars, born too young for one, too old for the other. In the Legion Hall he was sullen and tough, and seen to be that way. He was a soldier who should have been. But wasn't. Wasn't was what all these men were. Hedrick Platt wasn't dead. Alfred Walls wasn't sane. Bill McGriff wasn't the hero he said he was. Jaylord Hook, like Isaac Swinson and Telford Coyne and Luke Peddle, wasn't with us any more. They were all solemn and soft-spoken about any one-time soldier who'd at last died among them, solemn about their parades and flags, solemn about themselves, and bitterly willing to snarl at almost anyone, but there was no sneering, no loose cheap talk about the pain, the actual pain of a man, a soldier, who'd left a leg behind in the earth, the pain, an old man whispered to me one night while daddy was licking the point of his dart again, the pain you feel down in the leg but when you reach to touch it, it's not there, so you come up with only a handful of empty trouser, empty air, nothing. And this is just like the women who don't talk about birth pain, but are only glad their child got out alive, into this world alive. To breathe the air, the air as I stood on the porch that was now black with rain, a rain sheeting down, turning the yard to mud as Emma Easley was almost gone out of sight, no more than a pale wisp of a body in the rain, in the rising ground mist. I was standing barefoot on the porch

and then I stepped down into the rain, and soon I was up to my ankles in mud, soaked, my hair matting, the heavy drops like bursting petals on my face. The wind-blown rain came in long sheets across the field, drenching me so fast that I threw my head back, giggling like when I was a little girl. I was excited. I peed outside for the first time since I was a child, squatting on my haunches, and when I was finished peeing, all soaking wet, I stumbled forward a few feet and kind of sat down in the mud, rain water pooling around me, and then I began to haul handfuls of mud up my legs and then along my thighs and over my belly and breasts, pressing the mud through the wet cloth of my dress and then smearing my face so I could taste the mud on my palms, and smell something like sex in the mud, except it wasn't human sex, it was rank and sour like a mare when she's wet. I sat patting the mud into my hair, trying to mud-pack my body against the pouring rain till at last I just lay down flat on my back and I was so content that I could see myself sinking down deeper into the grip of the earth, into the musk smell and the skunky smell, sinking down into the antlers' embrace of dead animals, into the bite of their bracelet teeth, the windsucker bite of the dead, my dead parents and grandparents, hanging on like pitbulls and drawing me deeper and deeper into the rooted earth, into the tangles, where I was sure I would feel in the nerve endings of the roots the pulse of all my people who'd been put down, a pulling like the dull throb of a battery wire, and I lay there in the rain, slowly sweeping my arms fuller and fuller of mud, feeling the throb of the words of all my dead like maybe a deaf man feels music and learns to dance, pushing my fingers down into the earth, clenching, clutching as hard as I could on to something way down, way back, something as intense as the black light that shot through Evol's eyeball and the apple trying in his throat to outrun the rope when he hung himself, and all my people trying to outrun the dark and come up through black waters into the light, and I could hear myself crying

"Evol." I saw him sitting there on a flat rock threading the orange teeth of a beaver he'd dynamited out of a beaver lodge, threading the teeth along a line of chicken wire, making a necklace for Loanne. But all I heard was laughter. At first I didn't open my eyes. Then I did. It was Lute, standing over me behind my head. He laughed and laughed. There I was calling out to Evol looking up in the rain at the man that I'd not only bedded down but had just the day before legally leased all the back lots of my land to, all the back hills and mounds, and he said

"You got a gift, you got a gift for the rapture."

"I got a gift for making a fool of myself," I said.

"Naw," he said, "we're a pair, no doubt about it, that's what I was thinking just now while I was stepping off the backhills before the rain, we're a pair,"

so I picked myself up out of the mud and got into a squat, like I was a mud hen, and he got down behind me on his haunches so that we were even and he could knead my shoulders and neck. He liked to do that. I liked him to do it. The rain stopped and the light began to leak back into the sky and I do have to confess that it is pleasure that first brings a woman's heart to loving if not to love, and for me the first real pleasure is the smell of a man, the smell of his body, not sour sweat, but like Lute, who had on him this smell of the leaves of wild flowers, the dusky dusty smell of the

leaves because the flowers that're wild around here
don't smell, and on the other hand, Evol smelt of wet
grass and rosemary. I told him about that once and he
said no man could smell like rosemary and he went
and washed himself, which made me think that maybe
most men don't trust their bodies which is why they're
so hard on women because women, no matter what we
say, we are our bodies, the smell of ripeness and rot. I
used to lie cradled into the crook of Evol's chest and
arm and just breathe in rosemary and wet grass, the
grass he's now gone under, but he is never gone from
me because no one ever grows easier to love than the
dead, so I found myself blessed in both worlds, plea-
sured by the living man Lute and loved deeper by the
dead. "My mind may be thinking alone but it's never
on its own alone," which is what I said to Evol who
was talking to me inside my head the whole time while
Lute was doing his damnedest in my bed to drive the
demon out of me, since he insisted over and over that
Evol was a demon, saying, "A devil in mind is a devil
in kind," but Evol had already told me over Lute's
shoulder with that hard smirking tone of his that there
were no demons, and there was not even a hell, but
only an endless whiteness the color of drool or cum or

paste, the gruelly paste we used to make when we were kids, a paste out of flour and water to glue down cut-outs of movie stars from the magazines, pasting them into big floppy scribbler scrapbooks marked STARS, and Evol told me he knew that wherever he was in all the cold whiteness woven around him, there was also a distance that went on forever because he could feel for the first time in his bones an actual presence of forever. But he couldn't see into it, or through the closeness, which he said he somehow knew was the mind of God, and that was why there was no hell, because everything there is was in the mind of God and whenever he talked to Loanne, he knew he'd seen one thing for sure, that the mind of God was no child's rattle like he'd hoped for and he was no tiny stone clattering around in it. Loanne, he said, would suddenly come upon him out of the cold whiteness, not moving at all as if she had somehow always been there, and though he was actually seeing only her heat, like a fire that didn't burn but stung his eyes, it was a fire when she was gone that left him with an awful aching aloneness, not the aloneness he felt ever since he was without me, but an aloneness because there was no color, only a blur of something that he knew was nothing. Otherwise he was happy, happy to be left by himself, and unless I bedded Lute, Evol left me alone too in silence

but I yielded to Lute like a natural woman, though I loved Evol like I never loved Lute. I never did let Lute put his ear to my heart, though God knows he laid his head on my breast almost every other night, making me breathless when he touched me, laying his soft hands on me so that I shivered, wetting his finger-tips with spit and rubbing my nipples, but there was also something fierce in him, something so single-minded and relentless in his desire to exhaust me, to exhaust himself in exhausting me, that he seemed sent to ream every last feeling out of me, like he'd driven out my soul, and I wondered if my soul would ever come back. When we made love I had this feeling that I was collapsing inwards. I could feel my bones strain-ing, trying to hold what wasn't there, maybe my escaped soul. So every time I took him into me I was so alive I could scream and did, but also I screamed because I was afraid of dying, since all my blood seemed to disappear out of the veins in my thighs, leaving me dizzy and sometimes crying, "Yes. Yes," not only because he could touch me in my blood endings but because Evol was talking a blue streak in my ear, never mentioning what I was doing with Lute, although once I heard him whisper to Loanne, "Your mother's messing with some lunatic named Lute," and I was so shocked that he would talk to our little baby child about me that way that I said, "Shit," and then said nothing. I went stone cold and silent, which upset Lute, because he heard me. "What d'you mean, shit?" he wanted to know but I refused to answer. Evol said nothing, either, so right away I wondered whether I hadn't maybe made it all up myself because I have sometimes found while sitting out on the hillside or in a dark room that I overhear myself talking. I just suddenly find that my thoughts are on the loose out loud instead of inside and silent. Then I get a little frightened because it's one thing to overhear other people, including the dead, who are talking, but it's another to suddenly overhear yourself, so I try hard to keep track of when I'm talking out loud, especially as there's all kinds of things I wouldn't want Lute to know because a man in your bed is not necessarily the man in your heart, and since Evol was still in my heart I secretly wanted to know what he thought of me and Lute because I was coming to see that the Lute in my bed was a man I had read somewhat wrong believing he was a person hobbled by his own cross-purposes. But soon I knew for sure he had a single deeper intent to what he was doing, far more than he liked to let on. His pockets were always filled with gravel while his fingernails were pared clean, making it clear, with his soft puffy hands made for pleasure, that he was no man of the earth though the land was nearly all he talked about, how the land had already been bountiful to him, while he sat picking at his nails with his little pearl-handled pocket knife, pushing the cuticles back to those half-moons in the nails, his hands spread wide on the kitchen table, holding down a survey map, or suddenly when a great sadness took him, a wondering sadness, like he wondered why water always tasted so brackish to him, he'd put his head in his hands, the nails trimmed so close to the bone that you could see they had bled but I didn't notice the blood until he laid the land lease papers out on the table for me to sign, giving me what he assured me and I knew to be true, fair money, and it was money God knows I needed, money for the right to take the gravel out of the mounds and the big hill on the back lot and the slope behind the wetland pond me and Evol had dammed up, but right there and then, as soon as we

signed the lease papers, things seemed to hang in the
air as if everything had changed but nothing had happened, which at first was not so strange because
absolutely nothing does have a way of happening
around here, which is how Crudup's Mobile Home and
Trailer Park had appeared, a slope of ragged-ass hill
down to the river. It's the place where Emma and
Albert Easley had set themselves down along with
twenty or so other local farmers who'd sold their home
farms and parcels of land so that they could be unbur-
dened and free to move, buying big long trailers, squatting themselves together beside a shit-creek like
Crudup's branch of the Saugeen, stripping the running
wheels off the homes and setting them up on concrete
blocks while leaving the fifth wheel on the back-end
just in case they ever really went anywhere, or had to
make a getaway in their dreams, and some I've seen
even have one and two room additions welded and
bolted on, so I'd say a whole amount of nothing has
happened around here, nothing you'd like to pick up
and point to with pride, though Lute, looking at
Crudup's, had a different notion, saying he believed the
Park was a sign that the local backslide into poverty
was on the mend, that the good Lord was working in

mysterious ways, and we were on an upward tilt, about to be bountiful, due to the fact that people were facing hard facts. He had no doubt about it, being the only man I ever met who never did doubt the way his world was working out, which was the way he made love, because he figured everything was working to his favor, fierce

but it began to seep in on people that something was very much out of favor. It began at first only as a word behind a hand, but Lute himself whispered to me one night that terrible things were being done, that someone in the dead of night was attacking horses, horses out in the pasture, or sneaking into barns and slitting open their bellies, letting the guts drop out, sometimes cracking the horses stone dead with a hammer blow to the skull, or sometimes just going for the guts so that when it reared it pushed all its entrails out causing anybody who saw any of what was drained and spilled out onto the ground to get raging sick, wanting to shoot a man who'd do that, a man probably gone lunatic out of some long time nightmare, a man slinking through the dark with a knife he'd whet-stoned himself, some fearsome thing quietly worming its way out of his mind, or maybe it was a demon, one of those ebony-boned creatures with eyes for breasts that Evol's father had believed in, which would make the dead horses easier to understand, except no one believes in demons now, no one believes in the night-mare bogeyman so we're just stuck with the night-mares that stare you straight in the face in the daytime. I set out for the other side of the back hill worried and fretful about the back-hoeing and scraping and goug-ing into the hill that Lute and Albert Easley had begun that morning, the gouging out of the gravel. I went down into the swampy wet land through the cluster of bush willows and wild plums, following the creek through the dead elm trunks that were bound up at the base by dry long grass that had braided itself into the rushes, and I saw at the foot of the steep slope behind the wide black pool of still water which had formed under tall trees casting so much heavy shade there was almost no ground growth, a jutting triangle of three long poles in the shape of an arrowhead. And I had the sudden conviction that in this country of stone pickers the real scab pickers had got loose, swarms of black flies coming on in their wake, fly bites, and stars of pus with a fever lying in somebody that had broken like an egg, and the chill I got was like the chill I'd felt first thing that morning and had tried to blame on the ground mist when I saw that Lute had come over the rise of the concession road perched up in the catbird seat of a clanking, clattering yellow machine with steel treads and a great long belt that angled up into the sky over his head. Standing down below Lute, like he was standing on a ship's deck on a local calendar from *J. W. Grace Motors, Knock,* was Albert Easley, holding onto two long knob-handled levers. He was unshaven but he smiled his grim gap-toothed smile at Lute who cranked up the machine as it passed down the lane, churning stones and dust through the flapping plates of its treads, moving like it was a steel yellow insect with one jointed leg lopped off, a gouging machine finally coming to a halt at the base of the first mound out behind the fenced-in glass garden that was gone wild because I never went into it to tend to the flowers because I was afraid of cutting my ankles and feet on the jagged glass sticking up, and Lute climbed down out of the perforated steel seat and said

"Well, everything in its own good time, that's what I like."

He came back to the house and up onto the porch and chucked me under the chin, smiling like I'd never seen him smile, and I had this queasy feeling like I'd done a deal with a sly cunning man instead of a good come-by-chance preacher, a man I suddenly felt didn't care about me at all. He hollered out for Albert to get down and follow him, saying that they should walk up to Crudup's to the Easley house and see if Mrs. Easley was feeling better and would want to walk out on such a fine day but Albert declined and said he had to get started or he'd never get done and if he didn't get done there'd be hell to pay and the one who was paying hell was Lute himself, who looked back at Easley a little queerly and then smiled at me and stepped down from my porch while saying he wanted to know why I hadn't gotten around to planting sun-flowers in the glass garden, or for that matter in the front field that ran down to the concession road, a field we'd never used for anything before except a little hay-ing, and so he left me there thinking about sunflowers and the hint of meanness in his tone, and while I was staring at the back of him, and then at the back of the machine, I saw there was a big corkscrew churner for chewing into the earth and I felt a cold panic I couldn't quite locate, a warning shiver, though it was humid and hot and the air was loaded with dust. I went in and sat for an hour in the stillness of the house and then decided to walk out, passing Albert Easley out back behind the hill, the deer flies trying to tangle in my hair. I was swatting at my head like a damned fool to get them away. As I came down into the wetland, into the sudden mildewy coolness under the tall willows that stood around the pond, there were the poles, angled out from the bottom of the slope, and draped over the poles there was the hide of a freshly skinned horse, with the boneless legs dangling down from the poles, like torn strips of cloth weighted by the hooves, and the head was set out to look forward and bold, yearning for something up ahead and I wanted to cry, I just wanted to sit down and cry, feeling all tired and tuckered out, and I wanted to cry not just for the dead horse, but because of the yearning poke of his head into the gloom, like he believed there was somewhere still to go. I walked around in circles for a long time, revolving around and round, trying not to bump into trees, moaning to myself, feeling the ache of something churning at me, a tightening pain across my brow and belly, taunted by whoever had hauled that horse back into the woods to drape it over those poles, all my dead suddenly big as life in my mind there on the land my momma and daddy had cleared, the wetland that me and Evol had dammed for the birds and wild fowl. But then, the more I stared at it, there was also something calming about the still, hanging presence of that chestnut skin draped in the air and it took hold of me, so that standing and looking up into the horse's long snout and long yellow teeth, that boneless body struck me as a sheltering place. I hunched down and went in under the head and shoulders and then squatted and sat, staring straight ahead into the pond that was as dark and shiny as the ebony glass beads my mother used to wear, the beads she'd worn in the afternoon when we all, except for Evol, had gone back to the carnival and I was so pleased then to see momma and daddy happy, almost to the point of holding onto each other while they stood waiting along with a line of children to get into the little basket-chair on the ferris wheel, the wheel all crystal white in the brightness of the day, in the still heat that was strange for a spring day, a stillness that should have been a warning, but it wasn't taken as such, not by anyone. I was too pleased I guess by their laughter as they rose up into the air, the wheel rolling, the chairs rocking gently, and no one saw the funnel till the very last moment as it swooped out

of the southwest looking like one of those sting-ray
fishes in the air, dragging its tail as it swerved past a
stand of woods and bounced and tore directly through
the ferris wheel and the carousel, the whole carnival on
Kiln Korner exploding into spars and torn canvas and
splinters of wood and steel, and children like raggedy
dolls and wooden ponies and momma and daddy, him
with his hand in the air, went slowly looping in their
chairs, out into the air, except it was all over in a flash,
everyone and everything swirling for a moment before
they fell through the cloud of dust and debris like
stones, falling close to where I was still sitting on the
running board of one of the Indians' flat-bed trailers,
not twenty feet from the edge of the swath the funnel
cut through the carnival, momma and daddy dead for
no good reason. The next day, the newspaper said SIX-
TEEN KILLED BY FREAK TORNADO: FOURTEEN CHILDREN DIE,
and one of the carnival workers standing in the litter of
rubble and breakage, said, "It seemed like the end of
the world," but sitting in the still cool gloom, under the
skinned horse, I didn't hear horses' hooves or the end
of anything. I felt soothed, like I hadn't been since long
before Evol killed the trucker. I didn't mind where I
was, under the horse. And I knew I wasn't talking out

loud, but even if I was, it didn't matter. I was so safe by the black pond that I felt like laughing. I thought I'd like to laugh in my sleep. It was so quiet I could hear deer mice in the leaves, in the fallen logs. Ground vermin. And a still pond of ebony water. The horse was laughing. With the straining pull of his loose lips back from his teeth, he'd laughed as his throat was slit, and I sat calm and unafraid, sheltered by the hood of the horse, his hide scraped clean.

Chapter Four

For three days I kept to myself, wrapped in my grandmother's old goose-down comforter, lying there studying my mind and watching the hours go by like I was stepping on stones to cross a creek. I wasn't sick. I had laid myself low with rage and the longer I was lying there, the angrier I got. The angrier I got the longer I lay there, sometimes waking in a snarl of blanket and comforter looking for my shoes but then I'd drop back onto the bed and let my shoes be wherever they were, empty shoes under the bed. I could've spit at somebody but I swallowed back all my spit because I was maddest at myself for looking right into the downwind of deception and being too dumb to see the dimension of it. It's a hard thing to find you've been dumb in your own bed. So I lay there in the stillness listening to noise making its way through the house, trying to read the noise, the creaking and stretching of old timbers and the shift of loose glass in the window frames. Loose glass in the wind. Sounds I could feel, like Evol felt birds walking on his skull, like you hear when you've got a crick in your neckbone and you turn real quick to look at a bird falling on a downdraft. Evol heard birds all the time. And when he saw birds sitting in a row on a telephone wire he said they were listening in on the party-line. He always planned to train a crow to come to him, to come when he called and sit on his shoulder and I think that's how he saw himself sometimes, standing with one of his dogs, and a crow gabbling on his shoulder, believing that birds could talk to dogs the way he believed dogs howled at night because they could see the dead. He said a Chinaman had told him that but I don't know where he ever met a Chinaman. I heard Evol howling one night but I decided there was nothing to it, that he was drunk, but maybe he'd seen the dead, maybe he'd seen himself dead, though whatever it was, I had his dogs shot after he hung himself because I didn't want them howling about how they could see him. It's enough that I've got him nestled in my ear without having to listen to his dogs too, though he's never spoken to me since then about my killing his dogs much as he loved them, and though they were mongrels he bred them as best he could to fight to kill, but also he taught them to love him, and they did love him. They curled on his lap from the time they were pups, and before Loanne was born he'd let them sleep in the house, the two of them, and in the morning they'd crawl out from under the kitchen backstairs and come to the bed and try to lick his eyes open, which always made him laugh, and he'd get them to leap up onto the bed so I had to stare into the deadball eyes of two mongrel pitbulls, nuzzling like spaniels, snuffling in Evol's ears because he trusted them, he trusted them like a baby, though they looked at me like I was an open wound, and he'd smile that sly smile of his and stroke my thigh and sometimes stroke himself and then you could see their nostrils flare when he did that, their ears flat back against their skulls, and I'd hear a low growl, and I tried to think of something easeful and soft, I tried to think of my daughter but I couldn't hold her to mind so I lay there watching Evol stroke himself, thinking how strange it is to watch a man excite himself, his whole body rooted like he's been bolted down at the hips to the bed, holding the root, and sometimes I used to slick him down with Johnson's pure baby oil to get the sheen and the slipping easeful sound which put me in mind of when I'd watched the covering of mares on the Teale farm, the mare tethered with her tail tied up and grease slathered on her, waiting for the stud horse, his stupid screeching whinny and the curling of his lips away from his teeth, stumbling forward, hobbled by his huge wagging dong, which is what my momma used to call it. "Some men go ding and some men go dong," she said "and it's all church music to me." My daddy didn't think that was funny but she laughed out loud just like I laughed the first time I saw a stud high-stepping for a second on his hind legs, helpless, the hugeness of his dong swinging in the air like a gate rail, two farm hands slathering his cock and wielding him in, and the mare hardly seemed to care or notice but I came home dreaming of being tethered like that, wrists tied to my ankles, and mounted from behind, and I learned to kneel on my bed with a pillow between my knees easing my middle finger into myself, pressing down on the bonerise with the heel of my hand, settling on my haunches, squeezing, hardly moving, so different from Evol and the way he was doing, and sometimes I was so caught up watching Evol with the dogs watching both of us that I'd try to squeeze and cum with him, and though the two of us were so alone together there on the bed, you could almost call it a kind of communion thing, since what was so unsaid was being shared without a sound, not a sound except for the low growling of those lunatic slavering dogs, and I said

"Evol, do you figure we're kind of strange?" and he said

"Shit, it's all so crazy nowadays nobody knows how to be strange." He was lying back, cradling himself in his hand, as if he'd come full circle and home to whoever he thought he was, easing himself into a dream he had never wanted to end while he was stroking himself but had brought to an end as fast as he could, and Evol lay back relieved and so sad, dropping down into himself like a dying quail who was content-

119

edly helpless, and that was the only time I've ever seen him afraid, when his dogs started snarling and lapping at him, like his cum on his thighs and belly was blood, so he punched one dog so hard in the head that he broke the dog's jawbone, compelling him to put that particular dog down, shooting it in the back of the head which left him mopey and morose for weeks, not just because he'd lost one of his fighting dogs, but because he felt stupid, and Evol could not stand feeling stupid, though I've got to admit that it was times like that when I felt tenderest toward Evol, and I'd snuggle against him, talking a kind of baby talk to each other, a word snarl like we were holy rollers who'd got the gift of tongues, mumbling their words backwards and turning words inside out like children do, like Loanne did when she was just beginning to talk, lying in her cradle going *gawa gawa dayee dayee*, her pale pale blue staring eyes that she'd inherited from my daddy, who'd made me so afraid as a child because he'd look at me with those same pale eyes, eyes that weren't quite entirely cold, because their paleness was the color of blue petals, but they made me feel cold because I felt that nothing beautiful could live in there for long, not love anyway. The little I knew then about love. Maybe he was just low on the charms of love. It wasn't his fault that his laughter left us with the feeling of ice water down the back of your neck. And then, with him having no left arm after his accident, he shied away from folks to his left. Momma had a lust for him and always came at him on his right. She'd haul him into the bedroom by his good arm. Other than that, he and momma fought, they carped and wheedled, they filled the house with rages and refusals to give an inch. As I grew up I could see that they didn't understood their rages and they didn't intend their refusals, because they actually did love each other, if loving is not being able to let go, and they sure as hell couldn't let go. They'd latch onto each other with a word. He believed in the word. He had his dictionary, the words and words and words that tumbled all over the place down the page as he pronounced them and pronounced them, and momma riffled through the Book of Revelation like it was the original Farmer's Almanac. They could get their words going to beat the band but they had no way of talking to each other and I had no way of talking to them. I was sitting on the other side of the room holding the Bible, memorizing the names of the Old Testament Books, and he sat in his tub chair by the sideboard, reading that dictionary, two pages every night, pronouncing the words out loud. No one could turn on the TV until he was through pronouncing. Then he'd hand the dictionary to me, and I would read a page, any page, he had no plan, there were no particular words he loved. I once tried to read him a poem from a page in the *Farmer's Gazette* but he thought the sing-song rhyming was silly.

"God didn't speak in rhymes," he hooted on the December evening that he slammed the door in Evol's face for no good reason and staggered out drunk and laughing into a white-out snow storm, bucking the wind, making his way out along the shoulder of the concession road just as a big township snowplow came along and side-swiped him, the driver never knowing daddy was there in the blown snow, the plow-blade slicing him open at the shoulder so that he lay on his back in a snowdrift for a long time, passed-out and bleeding until the open wound froze. We heard the howling of dogs from the house and I thought of the dead and the Chinaman, but it turned out he was found alive because of the Teale's howling dogs. "The dogs thought he was dead," Evol said. "He's come back from the dead." Daddy was taken to the hospital and then he was brought back home wrapped like a mummy. I stood outside his bedroom door listening to him as he lay in bed saying over and over, "Jesus Fucking Christ Jesus Fucking Christ Jesus Fucking Christ," and to stop him from saying that word Evol said I should sit by his bedside, which I did for almost two months. I'd memorized the *Farmer's Gazette* poem, which I said to myself and then to him

> *Little Lamb, who made thee?*
> *Dost thou know who made thee?*
> *Gave thee life, and bid thee feed*
> *By the stream and o'er the mead;*
> *Gave thee clothing of delight,*
> *Softest clothing, woolly, bright;*
> *Gave thee such a tender voice,*
> *Making all the vales rejoice?*
> *Little Lamb, who made thee?*
> *Dost thou know who made thee?*

but he wrinkled his mouth and squinted at me. He liked to watch soap operas on the old Zenith TV, lying curled up on his good arm-side with one eye slitted open. He was of a wandering mind, mumbling words at me in a tangle of sounds, and half the time I never knew what he was talking about so I wasn't surprised that whenever momma came into the room he'd scream without warning that she was a goddamn SLUT SLUT SLUT. It was a word he seemed to like, to relish. It made him laugh, and sometimes she'd just smile this little snicker-smile of hers and she'd sit on the edge of the bed beside him on his armless side and unbutton her blouse and he'd calm down and nestle against her, watching me watch them like he was smug about what I was seeing. It was the only time I ever saw them touch each other with any open tenderness, though it beats me whether she was showing him love or showing him up because sometimes when he'd close his eyes she'd wink at me. With daddy in bed all day, momma took to doing nothing. She'd wake up in the morning and fix her eye on a hairline crack in the wall and then she'd go, "Haw haw haw," running her finger along the crack. Momma could hardly read or write but when she fastened her mind on a thought, she held onto it for dear life, she held onto doing nothing, going, "Haw, haw, haw," for six weeks. It was May and the lilacs were starting to bloom. She was slopping around looking peeved and he was half-dazed by boredom, but at last he healed and got up and started playing a game he called One-armed

Juggler, his trick being to have me stand on the porch reading the daily page from the dictionary and he'd toss a rubber ball from his right hand to the hand that wasn't there, laughing like his sides would split, yelling for one of Evol's dogs to fetch the ball but they were so sullen they usually took the balls away and chewed them up, which made Evol laugh, so daddy decided that eggs would be better than balls because no one had to catch the eggs and bring them back so he threw the eggs up in the air from right to left in an arc, making a shunting motion with his shoulder as if the arm was still there, but it wasn't, and pretty soon there were five or six blotches on the front grass, and then five or six more, the yellow of the yolk glaring, which turned my stomach, glistening smears in the grass for the barn cats to eat, if they dared, what with the dogs about, but daddy soon gave up his game and took to sipping whiskey again. He would sometimes weep. It wasn't like crying. It was weeping, sitting there staring straight ahead, wide-eyed and dazed with tears drenching his cheeks, sopping his shirt, wetting the lap of his trousers, like he was draining all the sorrow out of himself till a little smile crossed his lips, reminding me of Evol and the way he too would sit staring straight ahead, though he never wept but was also located in some deep sorrow that made him smile, like someone was trying to slip something by him, but you didn't have a ghost of a chance of slipping anything by Evol, who was always watching and waiting, sure there was something to see, something deep, expecting the happenstance of things to be hard, which is why he thought there was a well of tears deep down in the center of the earth, and after he died I sometimes thought about the whiteness of where he said he was and maybe he wasn't in the mind of God at all. Maybe he was deep down in his well of tears and didn't know it, and maybe when I'd gone witching on my land for water, feeling the tug of all the under-ground flow, I should have guessed that Evol, who never did cry, died without grace and was now in his purgatory, and one night when I was feeling sorrowful and mopey, lying in bed with Lute, I tried talking about Evol and the blind lady and my daddy losing his arm and the tears, but all he said was, "You better learn from your daddy. A man's got to watch out for himself when he's on the road alone."

"You better be careful," I said, wishing I could slap him on the back of his head. "Somebody could creep up behind you."

"And?"

"You'll be sorry."

"Nobody's creeping up on me."

"Don't count on it."

"I don't count on nothing, nobody's gonna creep up on me, because when I walk I walk like there's a wall behind my back even when I know there's no wall there." He said that whenever he was out in an open field he always felt there was a wall at his back because life happened like that, behind your back, unless you kept your eye peeled, and he had a peeled eye, he said, so peeled he could pick out a bird skittering in the long grass or in the crook of a branch, and sometimes when we'd gone walking over the land, he'd whirl around looking for that wall and there was nothing there, and he'd get real mad, and that's how I found out about the gun he had, his travelling gun he said, racked in a side panel of his truck. He was furious. He said someone was shadowing him.

"Maybe it's your guardian angel," I said.

"Don't be foolish," he said, and slipped the lock on the side panel, letting me see the high-powered rifle inside. He slammed a clip into it, stepped aside from the truck and blew a hole through the clear air, and then he blew apart a woodpecker that was pecking on a dead elm trunk, and then he took the top of the dead trunk off, too, smiling with an almost shy, sheepish satisfaction, saying

"Sometimes I turn around and I see a silhouette a long way out there behind me, like tinsel lines of light in the clear air, so faint and shimmering I can hardly see it but I know it's the shape of whoever's tracking me."

"Why'd anyone track you?"

"If I knew that I'd know who he was and I'd get him first."

"You've never seen him?"

"I never seen the Lord Jesus either."

"Maybe he's the one who's after you."

"Naw, I already sprung my heart open to the Lord and He is my light in the darkness we've got to deal with head-on. I have laid out my poisons. I have baited the sweetmeats and set them out, I have tasted the meat of sweetness myself, so I could take the tongue of the devil out of his mouth, so that when I spoke the good news would be clear, as clear as it is in the seed-grains of stone, for it is through the gravel and stones we shall prosper, and I have beheld the ladder set upon the earth and the angels of the Lord ascending and descending and the Lord said thy seed shall be as the stones of the earth, the seed of nations, and thou shalt spread abroad." That's the day I knew something dreadful was wrong because after that every morning at seven-thirty, Albert Easley came down the lane in that slumpwalk of his, going out into the back fields to get up on his yellow machine, or on his back-hoe, and he started piling topsoil like they pile dried blood in McRoody's Meat Packing House, with Lute standing on my porch on the third day saying to me, with his arm around me

"The earth's no good for nothing around here no more."

"That's not true," I said.

"Sure as hell is," he said. "No farmer's made a living off this scrabbly township for twenty years. Nobody you can name."

"I bet I could."

"I bet you can't because I know you can't. I studied up on this whole thing. The soil don't keep no one, not unless you get goddamn government grants. So then your whole life's on loan to the government. That's why all kinds of folks like the Easleys hauled themselves up by the hair and got themselves mobile homes so they could drive off to Crudup's and plunk themselves down like they were born again plumbers and carpenters. But we've got a blessing out here, we've got the biggest gravel fields anywhere on this here continent, all we got to do is scrape the earth back like it's dead skin, and it is, and then gather the stone seeds. I got acres of stone seeds under lease. Lease it. That's what God does, that's what He done. He leased us our lives."

After listening to Lute's trucks rumbling back and forth in the lane, the truckers and Albert Easley out there turning the mounds and high hill into open pits, after I wakened in the middle of the night hearing owls hooting and also all my dead, all my stone picker folks who were long gone and buried, out there howling like they were dogs because they'd seen the dead land that was to come, I called Burly Crudup, a man who knew about water, a man who'd handed me an abounding gift, and I said, "Burly Crudup, you get off your duff and show me exactly what's what around here," and he said

"What's what about what?" so I said

"Gravel, because what's going on over here would make a grown man cry."

"And what's that?" he said.

"What's going on."

"What's that about?"

"Gravel," I said in as easy a tone as I could muster for all the frustration I felt, since it was always so hard to ever have a conversation with anyone that went beyond the saying of the same words over again, whether it was Burly or my father, which is why in one way I was given to Evol and taken by Lute, the way they had a gift for talking, even if it was just talking at you, at least it was talk, and I said, "I want to see what's going on with the gravel pits I hear about, because of what's going on here on the Tull farm."

"And what's that?" he said.

"What's going on?"

"Yeah."

"Destruction."

"Destruction's a word a yard long," he said. He came by in the afternoon in his pick-up truck. I couldn't bear to look back over my shoulder as I came down off the porch, back to where Albert Easley was sitting squat in his catbird seat working the big backhoe. I lifted myself up into the cab of Crudup's truck and he drove off down the lane and said he was going to take me through Proton, Luther and Egremont Townships so I could see for myself that what was going on was ordinary as spit, and a good thing too, he said, because those folks who had nothing better to do might bitch about who was hacking down what, but no one gave a sweet damn for how the farmer was going to feed himself and after all, didn't he know that me and Evol had gone to the city looking for work because there was little or no work worth doing on the farms anyhow, nothing that would bring a dollar worth talking about, so a body had to do something worthwhile, had to figure out what the land could still give to a man on the get, "Like your Lute," he said, "there's a man who is surely on the get, because I see when most men are on the go he's already gone. I'd count myself lucky if I were you, falling under the hand of such a man, and a preacher, too. A preacher can always bring in a pretty penny."

Burly's cab was decked out like it was a tiny room, the seat being covered in custom-made zebra skin, and the dashboard dressed in crocodile black leatherette with chrome holders for the coffee mugs. The flip-down sunshields had silver tassels hanging from them and on the ends of the tassels there were these big rosy plastic nipples and when he saw me looking at them he flushed and tugged at his cap that had a sewn-on decal FARM AID, and said

"Got those at the Mortlake Dance Hall," and he reached over and flipped down my sunshield so I could see that up above the nipple there was a little mirror on the underside of the shield with a pen-light that came on.

"Here, you have a good look at yourself, you're a good-looking woman," and he winked and slipped a tape into the tape deck and started to sing along

> *Old Tougher-than-Leather*
> *Was a full time go-getter,*
> *The grass never grew beneath his feet*

as we turned down a concession road between Arthur and Damascus, a road oiled to keep the dust down, planning to drive around Damascus toward Luther Marsh. Some of the home farms we passed, with their old red brick houses standing lean as knives into the west wind, were gone to scrub willows and waste. Some were worked hard for rapeseed and hay, with rows of dead elms along the side of the road, the bark peeled and fallen away, but the weeping willows and the weeping birch were full and lush. Only the dairy silos were fresh painted, paid for by the Milk Board which bought all the milk and poured much of it into drainage ditches. Burly pointed and said

"Look at that right there, put your eye on that."

"Where?"

"There, that stand of bush back off behind the house, that's a brainy man right there, a man I believe called Cashton, got himself a sugar bush, plastic pipes tapped into each one of them there trees, the big boilers out back of his kitchen, he gets your hundreds of cans of syrup, and with him working what's left of the land for gravel for the last three years, why you can't hardly find him in the wintertime with him being a snowbird in Arizona because Cashton ain't breaking his back, he's too busy going to the bank." And I could see that what was once more than a hundred acres of field was now all stripped into great wide holes with all the top-soil scoured away, the sand and shale packed into breadloaf mounds, and where the land was chewed up the holes were half-deep with sitting water, lemon yellow and slimy in the afternoon light, but Burly Crudup was beaming, and said

"That may not look like the most perky parcel of land you ever put your eyes on, but make no mistake, that's a money-maker, and I mean all that gravel got up out of there by your back-hoes and front-end loaders is cash on the barrel, the kinda cash that makes a man feel light on his feet, I want to tell you. And all that syrup in cans makes for sweet living. What you're looking at is sweetness and light." He was banging his fist on the steering wheel. We had slowed down. The plastic nipple on the silver tassel was swinging back and forth in my eyes. "Jesus Lord," I said, and he said

"Lord what?" and I said, "Lord love a duck." We both laughed so that we didn't have to say anything more. I had a truly sinking feeling, because I could just see Lute raising his hands up over one of these holes, righteous as all get out, saying, "Praise the Lord," and then getting off the land as fast as he could. Burly started to sing again

There are clouds in the sky,
Clouds of fear and despair,
A love like ours never dies,
Changing skies, changing skies

and listening to him, I couldn't free up my mind from the thoughts of wells of tears and the memory of momma staggering out the front door of our house after she'd seen daddy's face in the sink water. *Changing skies.* I wished Evol was still talking to me regular because I would have asked him what all this meant, or was supposed to mean. I couldn't ask Lute, since he'd made himself scarce out of my house once we'd done the deal, light-footing it across the land. I was getting angry again, full of dread like I'd been all week, and I'd tried sucking on momma's two stones but it didn't work. I kept thinking of Burly witching for water, a good man who had a natural born gift, and I understood what he was trying to say in these times when men were drowning who'd never seen a drop of water. I should've counted my blessings, but then I didn't know that you got no blessings if you couldn't count. I started counting and by the time I got to a hundred I figured I should be a happy woman, but by the time I got to five hundred I was mad as hell because we were passing another farm that'd been turned into a trench like an atom bomb had gone BOOM, leaving the burn and scorch marks of the wrath of God. It was not a scar. A scar can bleed, but this was a dry wound brought about by that lepper for the Lord, Lute, doing this to grandma Brodie's land, to Tullamore land. I was sitting there on the rag at all this blight when Burly said, "You know, my folks, way back when, they used to own the lime kilns, you know that? Crudup's Corners, when it was called Crudup's Kilns, right there on concession 11, lot 21 and there were lots of kilns all over the township, cause they were necessary. Necessary is what you got to do and they did it, hauling limestone to their kiln. I bet a girl young as you never seen a kiln, but the thing was you had to get a lot of granite stones for the base, stones that wouldn't break with the fire, and then you laid in all the limestone you could, and built the fire underneath and you kept that fire roaring in the kiln for three days and nights and you'd find the limestone had broken down under the heat of the fire into tiny pieces and powder, and that was your lime. That was your basic fertilizer but also your mortar for building and holding things together and that was your whitewash for making things look pretty, and that was your lime pits to make things disappear. Those folks tore the hell outta this countryside hauling limestone to daddy Crudup's kilns and yarding out the old woodlots, they tore the hell out of it just like today. Make no mistake, my folks and yours were stones no fire could break, and I don't plan to break or go broke. What's got to be done has got to be," and he was beaming at me, pleased with himself, with his life, upright and straight and bold and I found myself looking at him sidewise with a kind of wonder, which he took to mean I was having a good time, and the next thing I knew he'd put his hand on my knee. I didn't say a word and took no offense but I took his hand off my knee and put it on his zebra skin seat. It had been a time since I'd had a man touch me, not since Lute and I were locked in a silence late one night in July. There's silence that has its own sound. There's silence that's the calm before the kill, and that's where we were that late night, breathing like we were holding our breaths, and I was so aware of the smell of the hunger in his sweat, not a hunger for me but just hunger, that I found I was aroused and I knew he was too, waiting for me to touch him, but I began to touch myself till I was all wet and then he could hear me shuddering and he yelled

"What the hell are you doing?"

"I'm doing myself," I said.

"No damn fool woman does herself while I'm in her bed," he snarled.

"I ain't no damn fool woman."

"But you're doing yourself."

"Right."

"That's a sin. Don't you know a sin?"

"I'll tell you what's a sin."

"What?"

"You get out of my bed first."

"Gladly."

"Get out,"

and he got out, got dressed in the dark, and then stood in the doorway and said, "Well?"

"I'm carrying your seed," I said, "and that's a sin."

He stood very still and then he said

"That's the Lord. Psalm 127."

"That's a man who thinks stones are seeds," I said, "and maybe what I'm carrying is a stone."

"Whatever you say," he said, laughing in the dark, "but it's mine, I got my mark on you."

"Nobody's mark is on me, and who knows what I'd do."

"You harm that child," he said, and he waited a long pause, "and I will kill you. Make no mistake."

"I already made my mistake," I said.

He turned on his heel and was gone out to the lane, revving his truck in that shadow light before dawn that's like water with milk spilled through it, except here I was with the sun going down as I sat sick with anger in Burly's truck, passing more quarries and then we were out by the turn-off road to Luther Marsh.

"They call that there a sanctuary," he said.

"Who's they?"

"People who butt in."

"Who're they sanctuarying?"

"Birds. We got a whole marsh that's safer for birds than most folks are in their homes."

"Don't say."

"The only people who make any kind of crazy living now out of that wetland are Koreans. They come up here from the city at night in their vans and get out in the dark and pick worms. Picking worms is big business."

"I'll be a monkey's uncle," I said.

"I haven't heard a body say that since I last talked to my grandma and I haven't talked to my grandma for twenty years."

"Me neither."

"You knew my grandma?"

"No, my own grandma."

"What about her?"

"Haven't talked to her in twenty years."

"You can't hardly be more than twenty."

"I am more, a bit more."

"It's an itty-bitty bit then,"

and Burly, suddenly paying no attention to me, began to sing along again

> *Was it something I did Lord*
> *A lifetime ago,*
> *Am I just now repaying*
> *A debt that I owe?*
> *Justice, sweet justice,*
> *You travel so slow*

as we took a twenty minute drive along highway 89 toward Knock, the town the police had dumped me and Loanne in, and the whole time, when I could have used the relief of silence, Evol was in my ear, chastising and chiding me about letting myself go mugwumping around at the behest and bedamned of men like Burly, born with their brains in backwards. Burly Crudup, who'd spit in a dog's eye so he could steal his dish, and

Evol started yelling so loud over Burly's sing-along that my head started to hurt, yelling "Gut a fish. Gut a pig. Gut the land. Fat porkers like Burly, all sweat and suet on Sunday afternoon, picking dirt outta their toe nails while praising Jesus like Jesus was a half-wit boy scared shitless of anybody who had a hammer and nail and these guys," Evol said, getting a menacing sound, "they all got a hammer and are just looking for where to get a nail, like that hardware salesman of yours for Jesus with his bags full of nails, so don't ever put your hand outside the blanket when you're sleeping because that sucker will have the nail home before you can say Jesus Wept," and I said to myself so that Evol could hear, that if he didn't shut up I'd probably lose my mind, and god bless, there was silence in the cab except for Burly Crudup singing

> *The judge would not believe my story,*
> *The jury said I'd have to pay*
> *But to the rose in all its glory,*
> *Not guilty was all I could say*

as we drove through the gates of the Mobile Home and Trailer Park, and passed down what was a kind of main

street, since behind some straggly spruce and pine
trees, the trailer park was laid out in something close
to rows, with each one of the tin homes plugged in to
an upright iron bar that was carrying electricity. Even
in late afternoon, the park was still almost empty, what
with the men working out as roofers or handymen
plumbers, so it was the women who were in the Park,
which was on a rise that was almost a hill, and then a
gully running down to a shit-creek branch of the
Saugeen, a stretch of the hill scraped clean of all grass
or scrub, more a rolling mud flat than a park, twenty
trailers, the sun heating on those metal roofs and walls
and baking everybody out of their homes during the
day because it was cooler outside than in, and so most
folks left the Park or found a place to do nothing under
a basswood tree, which is where a clutch of women
were sitting as Burly parked his truck by the Manager's
Station House, a squat blue shack, women sitting on
plastic and aluminum lawn chairs, some five or six,
and one tall scrawny man with shoulder-length hair,
all of them hunched around a big board that was set
up on two small sawhorses, a great big Monopoly
board that some man with a bent for carpentry had
made and painted with all the right parking places and

a great big DO NOT PASS GO and GO TO JAIL in the corners, and these women that were playing the game, they were all tipsy after a long afternoon of throwing dice and charging rent, and sitting right behind Boardwalk was the big fat stripper girl from the Mortlake Bar and Dance Hall, looking like she had all the game money, orange $500 bills stacked in front of her. The aluminum roofs and walls were snapping, shrinking now that the sun was down, going off like little pistol shots. The fat girl was wearing big owl-eyed white glasses and a purple poncho over her huge breasts and hips. She had small feet too, which she kept heel-by-heel under her chair, wearing white rubber thong sandals. Another woman, thick through the shoulders, was wearing a lime green halter over what my momma used to call a pigeon chest, and also a floppy denim hat, and beside her, old Alberta Shave was wearing a John Deere Threshing Machine cap. The fat girl put down some red plastic houses, peeling off 500s and paying the Bank in the center of the board. Her boyfriend was standing behind her massaging her neck and shoulder muscles. Burly said with what I took to be true affection, "You all break my heart." He wasn't looking at me so I wondered what I was doing there, what I'd come looking for from Crudup. I felt this awful pain in my chest, painful because it was growing bigger and bigger. I slipped two fingers inside my blouse to touch the little scar that was there, that sometimes bled. It was terrible to be loved by my father. He said I broke his heart, looking at me with those pale eyes of his, making me stand outside with him one day beside the barn, telling me he should have had a boy, while they killed the horse. He held the heart up in his hands, the dark blood rippling down his arms, the huge heart still beating like a skinned bird, and then I passed out and slept and slept and when I woke in the morning there was blood on my bedshirt and in the bed from the tiny cut between where my breasts were going to be and daddy was standing looking out the window saying that he'd put the horse's heart inside me, and though the cut would heal, the heart would always be in me telling me how much he loved me no matter what he said and if I was ever untrue to him the heart would burst and I would die

and though the heart swole up time and again, I knew I wasn't going to die. It was a pain I had to live with even when daddy was dead, the both of them dead on the day they brought momma and daddy home from the ferris wheel. I laid them both out. Stripped them down naked and got two enamel bowls and washed them, washing momma first. I looked in the water in the bowl to see if my daddy's face was there. It wasn't there. So I dipped in the cloth. There wasn't a bruise on them, like they'd never fallen out of the sky. Her skin was kind of tough and crinkled, except under her arms and inside her thighs, soft and loose, like old gourds get when they're going watery and to seed, and as I slowly washed her I had the feeling I was washing myself, and I wonder if the woman that stood in the doorway when Loanne was dying wasn't my mother, the three of us women walking in and out of the mirror of each other's lives, tougher than leather no matter how many dead men's faces we've seen in the water, "And the only thing," my mother said not long before she died, "is that it's not the disappointment that wears you down, it's the hope." I wanted to cry because of her long bony feet, the long yellow toe-nails curled under her toes, I kissed her on the forehead, kissed her goodbye

and then washed daddy, which I could hardly bear, washing his sewn shoulder where his arm should have been. I thought of trying to open his eyes, to see if the paleness had deepened into a color ready for seeing his way through the earth instead of the sky. He'd had sky eyes. But he'd never flown till the end. I sponged him down carefully, his face, his neck and shoulders and belly, his thighs and his sinewy legs, his knobby knees, and then I held his sack, his small seed sack, and his still, white cock shrunk back and small into itself, into his body, bloodless

and I felt the heavy pounding in my chest, and picked up the tattered dictionary and let the pages fall open and began to read over his pale face, and then I put the dictionary down on the pine table, on his arm-less side, saying "Leviticus, Deuteronomy, Exodus, Samuel, Chronicles, Numbers." I went to the closet where they had kept his blue suit and her white dress in a box and I touched my chest, touched the pale thin scar. It was wet, blood on my fingertips.

CHAPTER FIVE

THERE WAS A BOY IN SCHOOL WE
called Killjoy who had red hair and one eye. Not a single eye, but one good eye and one bad eye, born to it
that way, the lid of his bad eye drawn shut and tight all
his life, so when he looked at us with his good eye we
thought it was the evil eye, and if someone he looked at
got the mumps or broke an arm, we'd write on a barn
wall or in the dirt of a window pane that KILLJOY
WAS HERE. He was never here, or hardly anywhere

that anybody could see because he didn't want to be seen, but we always had the feeling he was close by. Sometimes I'd hear a warbling echo coming across a field, kind of like laughter like a loon was calling, but there was no lake large enough for loons nearby, so maybe it was Killjoy or maybe it was the devil himself. All of a sudden one summer a child got killed, shot. Right in the head. No one heard the shot or saw which way it came from but the child fell down and folks ran in circles around the dead child, and then they wheeled and flurried away, panic-stricken, but some of us thought we knew who it was, and wherever he was shooting from, he was shooting from the heart. He meant to kill, sitting beside us in school, bland-faced, but keeping his head down and shying away with his tight eye. My momma said it was the Droop Eye, a sign that he'd seen his own death inside his mother's womb, but the way I looked at it, it was too tight to be called a droop, it was more like a hood, a protection maybe for a blazing eye behind the lid. Maybe he'd been born with one eye shut so he wouldn't have to squint when he took aim with a gun, maybe he'd been born a perfect shot, his natural good eye having a scope's cross-hairs in it. I tried to look him square in his eye one day, looking for the cross-hairs but all I saw was a dark pupil like a bore-hole, deep, and he started to cry like any frightened kid, pitiful crying and then another child got shot and one of the kids at school said, "Let's not call him Killjoy no more, let's not write his name like that no more." The police kept searching for months for a gun and they even searched Killjoy's home because all the local children were whispering, and they also searched the dark woods and the fields, with neighbors who hadn't spoken to each other for years strung out in a line, holding hands and pacing the fields, but the gun wasn't found. Then the killings stopped. We left off calling him Killjoy and no child was killed or shot at again. People held their breath and waited, and waited, and then at last, breathed again. My daddy said, "None of them kids deserved to die. No reason in the world those kids should've died," but I knew in my heart that there was a reason, and it was a boy with one good eye who wanted the other boys and girls to stop calling him Killjoy and they did, and then years later, after the Dutch Elm disease had blighted all the tall elms, someone spotted a rifle high up in the throat of the barkless dead branches and said, "I'll bet that's Killjoy's gun." It was a gun but there was no way of connecting it to Killjoy, who was now called according to his real name by everybody, Albert Easley, who'd left school slightly balding and stooped before his time, and he'd gone on to become the local mailman. He kept signs posted on his family property for years: NO HUNTING! until he leased the farm to Lute. Then he'd moved with Emma Easley, who was a McCorkle from the next township, to Crudup's trailer park, to a squat house that he spray-painted gunmetal grey with flamingo window frames. He was still delivering the mail three times a week at the noon hour from his half-ton Chevy that had three silver trumpet horns on the roof of the cab. Otherwise, he worked for Lute. "A good man," Lute said, "a good man on the backhoe in the back fields." He said that because Albert Easley had gone to work on his home farm for Lute, gutting his own land. I went over and saw that all the back acreage was gone, stripped down to the bedrock, to where they couldn't stop the underground streams from filling in the bottom, building to a pool of stagnant and black water, all yellow around the edges, a yellow rancid-looking ring. I stood there and looked at that ring a long hard time, looking at what awful things Albert Easley had done to his own land, and he'd done it himself too, but otherwise he was no different from me and what I'd let Lute do to my land, to myself. "I did it for the good of it," Albert Easley said to me. "Lute's been a prayer come true." He and Emma Easley had taken to prayer. They'd entered Lute's church, The Chapel Of The Abandoned Apostle, and though I'd gone by the church of a Sunday and heard singing and what sounded like a whole lot of people hollering each other down, I never did go in. I'd had Lute in my bed but I didn't want to be in his church, except that like a witless fool I'd gone and got pregnant and I was carrying his child, at least three months and maybe gone four, so I thought I should go see what he looked like with his preacher face on, preaching. "DESTRUCTION," Evol whispered, like he was talking to me through gritted teeth. "That cornholer for Christ has been humping in your bed, and god damn, he's laid his seed between your bones, but that ain't the worst of it, the worst of it is what my daddy used to call rapine, and there is only one way to put a halt to rapine, you got to rip the throat out of it so it subsides down like a dog into the dust." I could feel how hard he was thinking, the coldness of it. Mostly, he liked to sidle around a hard thought and play the fool with his hambone slap on his thigh, particularly when he was cornering someone, whistling like there was no tomorrow, which there wasn't when he was like that. If it was the day of a dog fight, he'd break open a couple of twelve gauge shells and feed one of the dogs gunpowder and then he'd go out the door with the dog all sleeked up because he combed vaseline into its hair so it'd be slippery and I could see in the dog's eyes that he knew what Evol knew, and they both wanted it, which was blood, blood in the eye. "Here's blood in your eye," my daddy used to say when he was drinking and when he was drinking he didn't care if he killed or got killed. Evol gave his dogs the same chance, to kill or get killed, a chance in the sinew and bones that was there from the beginning, the way you can see it in small boys, boys the size of Evol's dogs. I knew a boy who bit the heads off of chickens. He sang in the All Saints church choir and bit the heads off chickens. That's how I'd come to look at Lute. He'd bite the head off a chicken if he had to. There was a fury in Lute, something that wouldn't let go. When Evol was training his pitbulls, his mongrels, he'd hang a deer haunch by a rope five feet off the ground and they'd leap up and clamp onto that meat and some of them could hang there for

Barry Callaghan

an hour and Evol said a pure bred, which he dreamed
of one day owning, a pure bred could hang for two
hours, so I figured Lute was a pure bred, a real windsucker who'd come to my door by some happenstance
but mostly by his own shrewd design, acting as sleek as
slick can be though I don't deny the pleasure I took in
him and the pleasure he gave me on the rise in the
dark, and even more, the gift he gave me of Evol talking in my ear, Evol who was now sprung so loose in
my ear that there was no need for Lute. Evol was free.
And I loved hearing Evol, though I couldn't figure out
why the child Loanne would want to hold back. I hardly ever heard from her, which hurt my heart because
she seldom spoke to Evol either, like she was feeling
sullen about something we might have done to her,
though God knows I had little enough time to do anything, little enough time before she died and Lute was
standing under the basswood shade tree intending
from the beginning to scourge all the workable land
around these parts, turning gravel stones over in his
pockets like some of Evol's folks turned their prayer
beads, which is why I said to him one day, "You're
turning these farms into a holy hell," and first he just
laughed and then he looked out over the back fields,

154

turning his head real slow without moving his body like crows do and got real serious and said, "You sound like one of them environmentalists, and I want to tell you, all that stuff's one of the evils of our time, because the devil always comes wearing the raiments of beauty, but I'm not fooled, nor is any righteous man of the Word fooled by the leaves that dress the trees, let alone the trees that dress the darkness in the heart of the trees. Environmentalism is nothing more than praying in the wilderness to pagan gods, and don't you think I haven't seen that abomination of a dead horse up by the pond, like you think I never learned nothing from the Lord, like you could get me to believe that everything that grows is alive with its own god, but believing that is above all the work of women, all this goddess talk, which is only worshipping of themselves, as if St. Paul had not said, 'The head of the woman is the man, the woman is from man. Therefore if her head be not covered let her be shaven.' Which is what they rightly do to women in wars who sleep with the enemy, shave their heads, because this is war. A war in which some die to save the many, like God told the Israelites to kill all the Midianites, men, women and children, to destroy them, and to us that seems a terrible thing to

155

do, but it's not terrible by a long shot. That'd be ten thousand people who would surely go straight to hell, but if they'd stayed alive and reproduced, then there would be one million people who would have to spend eternity in hell. So God in love, and that was a loving thing, took away a small number so that he might not have to take away a large number." Standing there listening to Lute I thought I should go shave my head and also shed his seed because I knew for sure that he was the enemy

and I thought of all the women who've sat in a hot tub trying to soothe themselves, staring into the water, wishing water was magic like some old folks said it is, trying to think about how to abort without an abortion. No single one of us wants to kill, we only want to cross over the killing floor, so much blood already on the floor, but momma and the women I'd gone to school with and grown up with had a host of home cures they could dole out if called upon and they got called upon a lot while I was growing up because as soon as winter started coming on we all sang, "When the dew is on the pumpkin, that's the time for dicky-dunkin," or if it was summer we'd sing, "Hurroon, hurroon the month of June, now's the time for midnight

scrooin," so there was many a girl who needed mustard
plasters applied to the small of her back while sitting
squat over a bowl of steaming ragweed root, or an
epsom salts douche every seven hours, or a syringe of
bleach if a girl had gone into the fourth month, or a
paste of bulrush seedpod pounded into pine sap and
boiled along with the root of nightshade and then
steamed together, for squatting again, or a douche of
white vinegar taken after swallowing prune juice laced
with Castor oil, this whole seed-killing shebang a sorrowful almanac of trying to break loose the child from
the seed pod, which is as good a way as I can think of
my womb, a child being a pea in a pod, hoping if you
were a scared girl that you could crack yourself open
between your thumb and forefinger, if only you could
get hold of the pod, though of course you can't, the
seed's got hold of you, but no matter because I had no
inclination to take any such remedies and cures. And
like Evol said, it's no wonder once we throw our seed
away we wonder why we end up like we do. I'd surely
come to loathe and even fear Lute, but just because I
loathed him and the child was half his, it was also half
mine, and I wasn't about to kill any single part of what
was mine, but in my night dreams I dreamed that I

might kill him, which was easy for me to mull on because Evol, who had said nothing at all in anger toward Lute's child, did have rapine hard on his mind. He did have a throat he wanted to rip open

and it was this rage, for all the loving in him when he was alive, that was terrifying. But it also drew me closer to him. It's hard to know what to say about a man who's got a gentleness he'll kill for. Evol was a man easily bored and he took the only cure he knew. He killed a man and thought nothing of it. He killed himself and thought nothing of me and my baby. Yet he's been gentle on my mind ever since. He bred mongrel dogs to kill and watched them get killed but kept on breeding. Yet I loved him. He was like a horse. His nostrils pinched like a horse's. And he could prance, and a prancing man is a dancing man and he knew how to laugh and whistle and play the fiddle and make love so you'd never guess at how deep his loneliness was, and still is, because all I hear in his voice now is loneliness, and no laughter, which means to me that he can't be alive in the mind of God like he says he is because if I was God, I'd have to laugh. There'd be nothing to do but laugh and Evol would have to laugh along too but as things stand, laughter's hard come by.

Sometimes I can't laugh so I try to ease up in all my thinking, to stop thinking, the way my daddy once didn't have a drink of whiskey for six months. He went dry as a bone. But it's hard to make your mind go dry. Thinking comes up from inside you as soon as you stop paying attention, as soon as you let your guard down, which is why I never have believed that anybody is ever what we call empty-headed. There are some of those concentrated folk who are none too bright, who maybe count their sums on their fingers, but they're churning away inside their heads anyway, like my momma and daddy churned the whole time. But I try to slow down, the same way Lute said he counted numbers to keep down his panic, so I tried rocking in a rocking chair, figuring that since all the old folks looked so calm sitting in rocking chairs there must be something to rocking, so I sat out on the porch in our old chair, rocking and listening to the radio, but that didn't give me no special calm, what with all the whanging and shouting that passes for singing and all the whistling bells and time-check stuff and fast talkers trying to sell things like a hundred baby chicks sent by mail to start your own chicken farm while I couldn't imagine anything more awful and filthy than a chicken farm, so I turned the radio off and just sat trying to catch the cool breezes coming across the porch, studying on how to get a steady rocking going, wishing I *had* planted a patch of sunflowers in the glass garden. And pretty soon I had the rocking figured out so well that I was having fun, rocking just like it must be on an ocean or a big lake, riding away back to the end-tip of the runners so that my feet were high up off the porch and then rolling down so fast that I had to brace my feet against the porch boards so I wouldn't shoot myself forward out of the chair, and I closed my eyes, daydreaming a sea beneath me that was full of fishes, a sea that was dark down at the bottom, and all the fishes were on fire with light, darting and doing curly-Qs in the dark water, puckering up their fish lips, which is why none of us girls would ever kiss Arnie Webber in school because he had fish lips, and the light the fishes trailed was like streamers in a dark dark stillness though I was up above rocking and rocking and laughing, not really knowing what I was laughing at and no sooner did a thought about Lute sneak up on me but I rocked back as high as I could go, almost tipping over backwards so that I didn't have to put up with even one thought that I didn't want, except after a while I

began to notice that the fishes were going out, the lights
swerving in the dark water were disappearing one by
one and though I wasn't thinking anything about it,
trying hard not to think, I couldn't help but see it, so I
looked longer and deeper into the darkness like I was
staring down into the black pond me and Evol had
made on the back acres, and pretty soon I made out a
big shadow, a shadow the size of a great big huge ugly
pike and it was slowly bottom feeding, easing through
the reeds and gulping down the light and I started
rocking and rocking faster and singing, "Jesus loves me
yes I know," at the top of my voice but I couldn't get
away from the shadow so I yelled, "Evol, Evol," and
the next thing I knew, just before I tipped over the chair
like a damned fool, another bigger shadow showed up
with a mouth as big as all of that darkness and the first
one was gone in a gulp so I sat half-sprawled on the
porch laughing, though most would think it was no
laughing matter, pike against pike, just like Evol's dogs
in the backhills barn where I went along with him one
afternoon, going to watch the pitbull fights in an old
barn on a farm north of Dromore village, a barn set
back in a grassy basin of marsh land enclosed by low
hills so that you couldn't be aware of the barn being

there unless you came up over one of the hills. It was one of the old barns that my daddy loved, since he had helped build a couple of them when he was a boy, frame and timber, with field stone foundation walls, proper barns, with all the mudsills and sleepers being of elm, he said, and tamarack for the rafters and basswood and poplar for the siding. Daddy had kept his own pike pole in our own small barn for years, the kind of pole they used, once all the timbers and rafters were squared for a wall laid out flat on the ground, to raise the wall-frame, and daddy used to tell me how it was to see the raised and joined frames for a barn like a skeleton on a hill in the bright sun with all the men who'd come together to build the barn sitting on the timbers as if they were sitting in mid-air, all of them being men close to the earth but uplifted for an afternoon, and he'd start in on the names of the best framers, Neil Penna and the Landrys, Robert Hawley, Ben Seymour and Joe Kabel and his sons, and the best stone masons, John Shearer and Henry Lauzon, and he'd start weeping, staring straight ahead, tears raining from his eyes. "Those were days of some real sharing," he said. "We had what you called beef rings. A group of us neighbors would butcher a cattlebeast and we'd all have a single white cotton bag with our name on it, and at the slaughter house everybody got his divided share on the morning following the butchering, and I mind we had it figured out pretty good for a fact, because after thirty-two weeks each of our families had got a whole beast, each beast weighing in at at least over 600 pounds, and the longest running ring I ever heard of around here was the Randall Ring up in north Egremont, the ring running straight on through for some 65 or 66 years but then with the coming of cold storage all that got to be a thing of the past and what was best of the past has been put in storage, too," and then to cheer himself up and change his line of thought he'd recite me a song, saying

> When I was in that railroad wreck
> Who took the en-gine off my neck?
> Nobody. Not a soul

and as Evol and I came down a lane to the backhills barn north of Dromore that afternoon with one of his little barrel-chested and bow-legged mongrel pitbulls half-starved and yanking at his braided rawhide lead because Evol never fed his dogs, except for the gunpowder, for more than a day before they fought, I was singing that same song

I ain't never done nothing for nobody

and he said he thought that was a good song and he started to sing it too, which struck me odd because mostly when he was readying up for a barn fight with his dogs he was so high-wired that he'd wince like he was in pain if anybody spoke to him, but he'd told me to come along that day almost as if he'd decided that I needed to see something, take something into the pit of my stomach and pass it through me like a purge, except it didn't pass through, it got stuck, but then maybe I was wrong and maybe that's what he intended because he was a wily one who'd hunch up his shoulders and tuck his head down just like one of his dogs, all the tendons tight in his neck, and as he strode up the ramp toward the open barn door, with the dog short on his leash, he looked like god's anger back before anybody was born, white-faced and pure, because there was nothing to be angry at, nobody'd done anything to him, yet he couldn't wait to get through the barn door to the ring, the pitbull ring, where other men were holding back their dogs on leashes and a couple of the dogs were blindfolded, scuffling their paws in the dirt, inching forward but then wagging their heads, trying to shake off the blindfolds, letting out thin whining howls that were part rage and part whimpering terror, and then they tried to bury their heads in their chests, trying to protect their throats

and once I'd got used to the gloom after stepping through the door, what I saw inside was gentle shadow slants of light slipping through the basswood siding, planks that had shrunk over the years so that hundreds of long threads of light made it look like it was early morning in the barn, a peaceable light, and the twenty or so men who were lurching and elbowing around the ring that was made of square bales had a look that at first took my breath away because I thought I was looking at the ghosts of Burly Crudup and Albert Easley and the Kabel brothers and other men I knew who'd come back into their bodies to be there, grinning at me, with this strained and drawn look in their eyes, drawing me down and back through layers of half-light to all those sweet men of my own blood who'd come up the corduroy Garafraxa road with seeds and sprigs of lilac in their trouser cuffs, clearing the land, always clearing and clearing and trying to get out in the open until at last, there they were, standing like Evol on a high hill, and what they saw was how dark their lives were and they gritted their teeth and settled for getting what they could out of life, or like Evol, they got out, or like Lute, they gutted what they could in a clearance that went way beyond stone picking, drawing stones and gravel up out of the earth with a vengeance when there was nothing to avenge. And maybe that made Lute even scarier. Saying all the great gaping holes in the landscape had a purpose, that once all the gravel was gone into the city the city could send all its garbage into the country to be buried, money-making fill for all the holes, and soon everything would be smoothed over and unseen and nobody'd know we'd ever been here and pretty soon I'd be making so much money I could buy myself a mobile home, like the Easleys', except all that garbage would get into the water tables and if I ever went witching again I'd be witching for poison. Whenever Lute got near to me now I was like one of those blindfolded dogs, full of rage and whimpering terror

because I knew Lute was no ghost, and I knew Burly and Albert Easley weren't either, the way they were hunkering around the ring in the center of the barn, a well-timbered place that had once been a pig barn owned by Isaac Shave and his family, who now owned the wrecking lot down by Crudup's. These were men who had learned how to knuckle down to need and necessity, all of them watching and betting on one dog about to kill another, the dogs suddenly sprung loose, snarling, their eyes bubbed out of their heads, short-legged and swerving in the dirt almost shoulder to the ground, charging off the swerve head-down and hitting a head butt that sounded like a rifle crack, bone to bone, their bodies bouncing back, squat for a second, and then lunging for the throat, slashing the flank, all the men yelling and hooting and cursing and punching the air around the ring as Evol's dog got in under the jaw, lifted, and grabbed the throat, clamping onto a rush of blood like a hose-pipe had been cut, the suddenly dying dog letting out a choked off high-pitched scream, and then a heavy glug sound that was swallowed up in snarling, with blood spewing up and blinding Evol's dog who let go and staggered in a circle, his left front leg somehow snapped, blood all over his snout. I'd seen nothing like it before except the headless rooster my daddy had scythed the head off in a drunken dance in the front yard, the rooster zagging and zigging through the garden that was now fenced off by plastic pickets and overrun by wild dogroses and broken glass, spraying blood, and Evol's dog rose up on his hind legs, his broken paw hanging, his body all red like a dwarf priest and you could hear all the men go silent, sucking air, shocked but excited, men who'd slit hundreds of throats and guts with only the blink that comes before boredom

and Evol, clutching a fistful of dollars, swept the moaning dog up in his arms, the blood smearing onto his face and shirt, and he carried the dog who was pawing with his good front leg at his eyes and snuffling to clear his clotted nostrils, off to the dark shadows of a corner in the barn where the water pipes and hoses were, and he hosed the dog down, washing the blood into the hard-packed mud floor of the old pig barn, and though I was shaking from the dog fight, in fact the ugliest thing I'd ever seen was watching pigs in their barn, all those big bristly fat squealing and snorting porkers and sows with their cold little pig eyes that were disgusting, disgusting I always thought because their shit is the only animal shit that smells like human shit, which is maybe why we accept that they're also more intelligent than any other animals, shitting and snorting pigs that'll turn from peaceable to cannibal for no good reason, turning on another pig, eating him to the bone while he's still alive, a crazed blood-thirst whistling in the air, snouts into the gut, snorting up full of blood and gristle, and there's nothing a farmer can do but shoot them or hope the blood lust doesn't spread

as Evol laid a small blue blanket over his dog and wrapped him so he wouldn't chill, and then carried him, cradled in his arms, out of the barn into the afternoon sunlight, winking and smiling at me, almost one hundred dollars richer, singing

> When I was in that railroad wreck,
> Who took the en-gine off my neck?
> Nobody

So I sang too, singing

> Not a soul

but I have to say, whether I was out at that barn or home alone in the dark on the porch watching fireflies,

I didn't spend a lot of time worrying about my soul. It had gone, fled, and for good reason. It was no fool like I'd been. Still, I'd felt all along that it was intact. It had to be. And I liked that word. It came to me one day, just like I'd heard on the day Loanne died that Lute was intended. There was nothing I could do about Loanne dying and little I could do about how Lute came into my life, but there was something I could do about getting him out, and as soon as I decided that, that's when I came to feel intact myself, feeling, as a matter of fact, that my soul had slipped back into my body, slipped back in when I wasn't looking, so I knelt down, not saying I was sorry for anything, I wasn't trying to say I was sorry. I was just kneeling down, not to feel humble but because I'd been through a lot and I was still me. I went to sleep that night and slept the sleep of the just, who my daddy had always said were different from the righteous. "The righteous'll kill you for your own good," he said, "and that's different from the just." He didn't tell me why the just would kill you, but when I woke up in the morning Lute was out hammering staked signs along the sideroad beside the mailboxes, and I came out and saw him with his claw-hammer in the air and a sign that said he was running for

Reeve right by my box: ALM'S FOR THE PEOPLE, and I said, "Get that goddamned sign off my property."

"But we got an arrangement," he said, and I said

"You got the gravel but you don't get all the ground."

"Without me you got nothing," he said.

"I got a whole lot. I got me."

"Wrong. I got you."

"Not no more."

"I got my child in you. A child of the Lord."

"In a pig's ear."

"You better watch out for your soul."

"You better watch out for yourself."

"I told you before, nobody's gonna get me. I got my eye peeled."

"Praise Jesus."

"Don't mock me, woman."

"I never seen a mocking bird. I think I'm going to come at last to see you preach a while,"

and I did the next Sunday morning. The trees had all turned honey and lemon-yellow and red and ochre and the turning leaves always had a settling force on me, turning me to reflecting, not at all about death because the leaves on the trees were dying but to the color of the leaves. I like to think about color. Sometimes I see words as colors, blobs of color or a pale drizzly staining across my eyes, I don't care, it's all color, and it comforts me. And sometimes I get surprised. When I was nursing Loanne and I talked to Evol about nursing, everything was a color I later learned was called puce, which is a pretty lousy sounding word, but when I said the word suckling instead of nursing, everything got electric blue, shimmering so strong I had to blink, and when I said suckling pig, playing games with myself, it all became a vibration of blue and white, and then one day I said pig all alone by itself and pig became the color of pig fat, pure white, the same color of white that Evol said was God's mind, so I decided I didn't want any part of pig fat or God's mind because maybe they were both the same thing, and though I still trusted Evol and whatever he said, I didn't want to be wherever he was, whether it was the mind of God or a well of tears, because maybe they were the same, too. I had my soul intact in me and I had another child and when I said the word child I saw honey, a dark honey color, almost an ochre, the same color that was in so many of the leaves dying on the trees, so the only way I could look at it was that the dying color

and the about-to-be born color were one and the same,
so that when one was happening the other was happening, when one was dying one was being born, so
the leaves dying on the trees in all these bright colors
were not like the last rise of fire before the ashes, the
ashes that call a bird of death down into a house, but
were a blessing on the bough of how it would be at
birth because after all, if the dying leaves were just
about dying, then they'd have been grey and blotchy
and pasty with lots of liver spots as a sign that the sap
was done. But the sap wasn't done. I wasn't done.
Life may be short in the long haul and death maybe is
in the back of my mind—and who could blame me for
it—but birth is honey, a sweetness after the sting, and I
have walked and can still walk the map of my land
like it was the palm of my hand, with all the darkness,
increased as it is, held in that crystal web of underground waters, and no matter the map of Lute the
mapmaker, the secrets of honey-making, birth and
feeding are in me. Each secret a magnolia. Intact. No
matter the intended. My momma saw the death face
of her man in the water, but not me, I don't see death
in the water, I am not on the side of dying though
dying has got to be done. Nobody has died in me, not

Evol, not Loanne, though they may be dead. They are alive and heard from. They are heard

and the morning I walked out to go hear Lute preach it was a morning of Indian summer that had come late, a sudden swell of heat and sun, the heat riding on a soft wind, the heat and wind so soothing that I felt brisk in my body as I walked at a good pace past the woods, all the trees turned to hundreds of patch-quilts of color and since so many of my words turned out to have colors then maybe all those colors were words, maybe the trees were full of words, fluttering, the last words for the living before the winter, and maybe they were words that only the birds who filled the trees understood and took with them in the winter, the loneliest sight I have ever known being a bird on a top-most bare branch, sitting, and then taking off into a grey sky, gone into the cold, cold coming on, and once I got past the woods to the concession cross-roads I could see in the air that had been cleared by the wind the gates to Crudup's trailer park and across the road, The Chapel of the Abandoned Apostle, a little yellow brick church, and on the shoulders of the road, rows of signs: ALM'S FOR THE PEO-PLE. There were cars and pick-up trucks parked on the lawn, nosing up against the cemetery fence, nosing toward the gravestones. The church doors were open. There was singing, the high-pitched singing of several women, his Carolers

> *Jesus Lord, my heart's entwined,*
> *Jesus Lord, in the holy vine,*
> *Jesus Lord, thou art mine,*
> *Jesus Lord, I am Thine*

I stepped up the stairs, late for service, and saw the old chapel pews were almost full of local folks, the women wearing broad cloth hats or flowered handkerchiefs and box suits or slacks and the men were pretty much all in the same powder blue or brown suits, the kind of single-breasted suit the bank manager in town wears every day, except his suit-coat doesn't button over his shirt any more because he's got too fat, so you get a lot of belly from him over his big shiny cattle-horn buckle. He was there, too, standing on the aisle at the front of the chapel, the walls of which had all been painted white, and the wainscotting too, but the altar walls behind the pulpit were powder blue like the men's suits, and there was a carpeted platform behind the pulpit and there were five women, including Emma Easley in the middle, on the platform. They were the choir and Emma Easley, wearing a pink knit suit, was pregnant again, or at least she had the stomach for it. She was singing loud and being beamish. Lute, standing in front of the choir women, wearing a pearl-grey suit I'd never seen before, with his hair close-cropped, started in to preach, talking real quiet as the women hummed behind him, saying, "The word of God is all too often not in the house of God because prayer has to have deeds of love behind it. Like Job, who got healed as he prayed for his friends, we must pray for each other because prayer availeth the righteous, Isaiah, chapter 59 — wherein the Lord looked for an intercessor and didn't find any," and Lute, who'd been preaching with his eyes closed, looking lost in a childlike calm, opened his eyes, throwing his head back, cutting loose with a cry, "So therefore he put on armor to bridge the gap, to intercede, put on what the Bible calls the bowels of compassion, and so we are able to go through the bowels, whoever is making intercession, whoever's doing deeds of love and compassion, healing himself and his friends. Therefore, it's all in the doing. We are get up and go people who get things done. We are people of prayer, and the deed of love behind prayer

becomes the Word and the Word today is — *Therefore*.
Therefore. I have counted in St. Paul to the Corinthians
the use of the word therefore 126 times. Sat down one
day and counted it. Over and over, the word therefore,"
and he had his arms outstretched over his head, his fists
clenched except for his forefingers, pointing, his eyes
squinting and his mouth slack for a moment, like his
thoughts had slipped, but then he said, tilting his head
to the side but leaving his arms upraised, "I looked it up
in the dictionary. What is this word therefore that St.
Paul keeps using? What is it? And what use is it to
him? And I learned that it's what they call a conjunction, and a conjunction is like a word that intercedes
between. One thing can't get to another without it. So if
you've got one thing and you want another thing to
come out of it, you've got to have a therefore, and therefore I say unto you, like the Lord said unto you, go
therefore and prosper in His word, prosper in His seed,
prosper in His deed as we pass through the bowels of
compassion in this dark life into the light," and he laid
his hands out in the air like a blessing, like a laying-on
of his hands, those soft, soft hands, and he cried out, "I
can feel the healing light here in this room, the healing
of a right knee, heal the right knee, Lord, like a brace is

going around it right now, heal, and I ask you, who are the Lord's children, to leap up and receive the prayer language, leap up therefore and say words for Jesus," and folks were rocking and moaning and praising Jesus, sweet Jesus, and staring at Lute and hearing the word Jesus over and over I saw black, getting blacker, like black glass and blacker like I was going to pass out, except I was crystal clear awake, and Lute was screaming, "Leap up therefore and say the word Jesus, leap up and receive the prayer language, whatever words you've got in your heart, they are the words to talk in tongues *hobunahagoom amunimunabla a moomgalaba* because the Lord don't have to hear you in English, He don't have to hear you in any language that means anything to anyone else, but He only has to hear the words you sound in your heart *analawallanball* and therefore let His word come to you in the same spirit, and you may not know what it means but it is in your heart," and standing behind Lute, Emma Easley was bawling out at the top of her voice, "*Chinamanodillyava, chalamana mananacha,*" her hands folded, like she was blessed and peaceable, across her belly, staring up at the new gyprock ceiling, and then she hollered, "The seed of the man of the Lord is mine," and I looked around quick for

Albert Easley but I could see he wasn't there. Maybe he'd flown the coop. When a buzzard takes off in the deep woods, or even more I guess if he was to be found in a church, he makes this *whumhfl whumhfl whumhfl* sound with his wings, and for those who've heard it, for those who've really listened for the true sound of the brush turkey, it's like no barnyard gabbler but just like the sound of a buzzard's wings taking off, exactly the call of one of Evol's turkeys that he sat in the woods waiting for, the sound of wings tonguing the air, except I thought of Albert Easley taken off somewhere and Lute up there gabbling like a wild gobbler for God, one more buzzard among buzzards, praise Jesus, and I saw shadow, falling shadow in shades of grey, the whole chapel, no matter the white walls and the pink suits and shining powder blue suits, seemed in a darkening light to me, and Lute kept repeating over and over, "Jesus, Jesus, Jesus, sweet Jesus," with his long arms upraised, his hands wide open till I thought the bones in his hands were luminating, laying his hands on the heads of women who were coming forward, sheepish and sort of bashful, like they'd been caught wetting their pants but wanted everybody to know they'd wetted their pants, and he praised the Tubular Bells and Chimes and held their heads pressed with his palms until they fell backwards like they'd been cold-cocked, back like I used to fall when I was a girl into the hay, sinking down and feeling all the heat that's held in a humped pile of hay, the ripe smell of wet-rot seeping up from the floor that made me drowsy and dreamy, and I used to dream of roses while lying in the hay mow, long trellises of twined roses stretching like ladders angled out into the sky, ladders for everyone I knew to climb up into heaven on, and the rungs were made of glass flutes played by the wind, but no one ever climbed the ladders and the ladders were full of beautiful music but they ended in a sky of dry whispering thunder and all the roses suddenly shed their petals and fell and fell as if the sky had been plucked clean of red feathers, turning, as they hit the ground, to wet flakes of bleeding snow, snow shrouding a man who was sitting hunched between twisted pine trees, a man shivering, my uncle Ambrose, who'd crept late at night to get close to the Carlson lime kiln on the concession road corner on a cold night in December, quietly drunk and creeping into the kiln for warmth, the kiln like a sleeping snug, the floor dark with all the charcoal fires underneath seeming to be out, and he went to sleep soundly only to be found in the morning, a skeleton sitting bolt upright, the arms upraised, all the flesh gone and the bones glowing red in the kiln darkness

and my momma said he should of known better, drunk or not, because he was a house painter and painters knew about lime and besides, he had a hump, a small humpback, and a hump was a sign of luck. She said, "Maybe his hump wasn't big enough for him to have luck all his life." When they touched his sitting bones with an iron bar the bones crumbled to ash and his ashes were later spread in what's now the glass and wild rose garden, but in a way I figured he was lucky because if Lute had seen that hump, if he'd decided there was gravel in it, he'd of torn the hump right off his back and left him to bleed, to bleed and pass through the bowels of compassion making sounds like a buzzard trying to take off, and maybe that is really the sound in the heart that God hears, *whumhfl whumhfl whumhfl*, the beat of my heart sounding like a scavenger bird's wings, trapped in my rib cage, and that's how I felt in Lute's chapel, trapped among the righteous

and though I may not be just, before Lute's service was over I fled. My feet were freezing cold. I was sure my uncle's feet had been cold, but this was Indian

summer and not the winter. I stood shivering on the
fieldstone stoop of the chapel, feeling like I'd been
chilled to the bone, looking for birds. I don't know
why I was looking for birds. There were none, none
that I could see or hear. The sky was an overcast grey
with a lustre to the grey like there was a sheen of light
inside it, a silvering sky that cut off the earth at the
ends of the concession road and to the east, over the
sharp rise, I saw a horse drawing a small black carriage
with a hood over it, a pacing horse making good speed
along the gravel road, and in the carriage a woman and
child dressed in black, Mennonites, and I stood there on
the stoop hoping that I had the halo of light around me
that Lute had seen, the halo that meant I wasn't going
to die, and as the carriage drew close I waited for some
sign, some look so I could feel free to wave at this
woman in black and her child in black who'd suddenly
come on through from out of the east, but she made no
motion, no turn of the head, holding the reins with one
hand and her black swaddled child with the other and
she drove on by as if I'd never been there

and for a dreadful moment, so dreadful I wished
I had two of momma's flat stones, I was afraid I didn't
exist, afraid that any halo of light was a light around the

ghost of myself, and only everyone else around me was real, and maybe death was so much on my mind because all along I'd been slipping through the silvering like those women we'd years ago thought were lost, disappearing into the dark woods, sending out in their stead Armenian traders to confuse us, as if anyone at all could come out of nowhere and never have to explain what they were doing here, and maybe that's where the horse killer had come from, and I wanted to yell at the woman in the carriage, "What're you doing here?" but she was well on her way behind her pacing horse and pretty soon she disappeared off the end of the road and all I could hear behind me from inside the chapel was Lute crying, "Heal, heal," as bodies fell over, collapsed into the arms of their neighbor friends, passed out and free of pain

but before I knew it folks were crowding out of the chapel onto the stoop and the grass and Emma Easley had her arm linked under mine, saying, "It ain't nothing false this time," and I said, "Good for you," and she said, "Good for us all because this here's a God child, same as your child." She winked. "Lute's a blessing," she said, "praise Jesus," and I said, "Praise nothing that you don't need to," and took off in my stomping

stride and didn't look back till I came face to face with
one of Lute's ALM'S FOR THE PEOPLE signs, and I
turned away and looked back and there he was waving
after me surrounded by folks who looked like they
loved him and I wondered why Evol had not had a
word to say all morning and then I realized he'd already
had his say and that's all there was to say being a man
of few wasted words and to the point. And I finally did
get the point, sitting by the narrow upstairs window
overlooking the scarred fields as the leaves fell from the
trees, as the colors turned brown, as the words shrivelled, the branches bare, stern as disconnected wires,
and a cold snap set in followed by freezing rain. The
branches were all sheathed in ice, like the glass rungs of
my ladders, and they even whistled in the high winds,
it was a good time for clear cold thinking. Things were
close to worst but I was calm, waiting for a sign. I
found I didn't need sleep. I stayed up with the hoot
owls. And I didn't eat much either, mostly bread. In
the mornings I took long baths in cold water, and I did
the same at night, wrapping myself afterwards in towels
and my daddy's old dressing gown, sitting before the
fire watching the eyes of the flames moving at the heart
of the fireplace stones that were so perfectly set that

they still seemed to float after all these years in the shadow light of the parlor, and I didn't drink any whiskey at all. I had a steady thirst for water from the pump, from the spring well that daddy had drilled decades ago, the well we'd all drunk from and been cleansed by, water with a faint taste of iron. One night I thought I heard Evol playing his fiddle so I opened all the windows to hear which way the music was coming from but it wasn't coming from anywhere, not any direction, it was just in the air, like it was a layer of the air, running against the wind in the same way that levels of water can run counter in two layers. The house got very cold with the windows open. I wondered what I was going to do for heating in the winter time. I wondered what I was actually going to do. I hadn't heard a word from Evol. But I knew what he thought. I worried about Loanne, whether she was lost to me, and whether I was lost to myself, although I felt a calm. So still that I sometimes couldn't hear my heart, and could hardly see the pale scar between my breasts, and sometimes I didn't know how cold the bath water was or how cold my body was, too

and then the snow came. Not a lot of snow, not much more than a dusting, an inch or two that would soon melt, but that meant the big snows were coming on and it also meant that Lute was coming, coming before the big snow because the last of what he wanted to get up out of the ground was still there, the last of the gravel was there under the long dark wetland pond and under the slope behind it, the slope ridden by the skin horse. It was the pond that me and Evol had made. The yellow front-end loader and the back-hoe were parked on the side of the pond facing the slope and on the day of the snow I circled through the marsh in the lee of the hill to a stand of birch trees and thick willow scrub, and crouched down at a distance from the foot of the slope cradling Evol's turkey gun. I waited and I waited all day. I knew what Evol had told me, that you never set out hunting and trying to track after a brush gobbler because you'll never get him. You wait for him to come to you, and if you know where his territory is, then he'll come on through in his own time, right on time. I waited all the next day, too, and the slick of snow had melted away in patches. I saw at the edge of the marsh bulrushes, a print, a webbed toe print, and maybe, I thought, Evol had been on by, but more than likely it was an otter. I'd just got back up into the cover of the clump of birches when Lute came walking fast around a

pile of broken scrub brush and boulders that Albert
Easley had built up out of the surface scrapings of the
last pit they'd dug. He had bundles under each arm
and he was wearing high, olive-colored fisherman's
boots and his blue plaid jacket that I'd first seen him in,
a hasty man when he wanted to be and he got into the
water without wasting time, hunching forward and
moving along the half-moon shaped rim of the small
dam, setting sticks of dynamite just like they were candles, tied and wired and when he was done he stepped
back into the black water and looked up at the slope
behind the dam and the horse, his hide mottled and
mangy-looking after weeks of sun and the wet weather,
but the lean head was still angled up in the air at the
end of the poles, stern, but grinning even more than it
had been. Lute stared at it, standing there in the water
with the wind swooping down off the slope and he
turned and looked back down the length of the pond,
like he was calculating, and I remembered Evol saying
as we looked down along the same stretch, "That's a lot
of water over there that I'm looking at," and I said,
"Yeah, and then there's all the water underneath," and I
almost laughed out loud again as I settled the gun into
the crook of my shoulder and held it steady, smelling

the oil I'd put into the works the week before. I held him in the sight a long time. I wanted to think through the words of what I was doing, not so that I'd change my mind, and not because I'd be damned to hell, because hell seemed to be in God's own mind anyway, since he had killed one to save himself from murdering many. No, I wanted to say clear and plain to myself what I was doing so there'd be no qualms afterwords, no quarrel in my heart. I heard my heart beating, the sound of wings, and I tucked the gun close to my cheek, closed my left eye, fixed Lute in the sight again, opened my left eye and saw Albert Easley half-trotting and stumbling toward Lute, splashing through the black water till they were standing face to face and started talking to each other low but angry because Albert Easley was in a rage, pointing at Lute, then pointing up at the horse head and then tapping his own chest until Lute laughed, throwing his head back and his laugh came up the hill like a lost dog's howl with a hoot in it, and it was like the hoot was a call, because behind them at the end of the black pond where the water spilled over into the marsh, lone men and women began to ease up out of the water, taking to the shallows, two of them straggling to the side, momma and daddy bent but going forward, and behind them a cluster of men and women, the men all wearing moustaches, looking startled, like it had been such a long time before coming home that they could hardly believe they were here, and the place where they were walking in the shallows had an amber lustre to it, like amber glass, and I kept looking for my uncle Ambrose to see if his bones had become his body again but he wasn't there, not in among the suddenly lunging cluster of men and women I didn't know, who were moving together as if they were scared, but how anyone among my dead could be scared was beyond me because there they were big as life, and one of them had to be great grandpa Tullamore but since I'd never seen him I didn't know who he was, so I decided he was the portly man carrying his bowler hat in the crook of his arm with the hat full of wild flowers, and as he passed Albert Easley, Albert pulled a gun out of his pocket and put it right to Lute's face, right to his forehead. "KILLJOY IS HERE," I said to myself and I crossed Evol's gun on my knees and watched as Lute smiled and put his hands on his hips, bold as brass, and then he spat. Albert Easley stepped back, Lute laughed, and Albert Easley turned and walked through the shallows to the end of the pond, looking back at my people like nothing was going on, like he was so tied up in himself that he was oblivious to my people passing around the dam and up the slope, and just as the last one, who I thought had the look of a Tullamore, got beyond the horse, Albert Easley squared himself in the black water and took careful aim with his arm held straight out. Lute suddenly yelled, "And his children are as children of the Lord." Albert Easley aimed, but not at Lute, and he fired. He fired at one of the clusters of candles. There was a thundercrack and a great spout of mud in the sidewall of the dam, and another crack with a light that was like sheet lightning in my eyes, the light swallowed by smoke. They must have heard that BOOM clear across the township, and when the earth stopped shaking and the wind coming down the slope had cleared the smoke so I could see the water that was rushing away into the marsh, I couldn't find anything of Lute, but Albert Easley was standing down at the other end of what had been the pond looking like his old self, one eye tight and slumped in the shoulders and wiping his brow with the back of his hand that was holding the gun, and I thought, "God bless Albert Easley," not because he'd blown up Lute but because he'd waited until all my folks had passed over the hill, which answered my father's prayer, because he had always said, "All I want to do is get out of this world alive." He was out, and my momma too, and all the other stone pickers. I watched Albert Easley follow the rush of water into the marsh so that no one would ever find his steps, no one would ever know he'd been there except me. But I'd always known about Killjoy. Though Killjoy didn't know about me. As he disappeared into the marsh I said, "The more sin grows, the more grace abounds." Not only was Lute dead, by my intent if not by my hand, but I had life in my belly. As I stood up, looking to find a way home, too, so that no one would know I'd been there either, so that everyone would think Lute had blown himself to Kingdom Come, I saw the halo of light not just protecting me from dying but spreading out to all I could see, so that everything before me was amber and silent, and I knew why Loanne had not spoken to me through all these months. She was waiting, waiting to be the word in the ear of my coming child, as Evol has been the word in my ear.